CHOOSING *Love*

CHOOSING *Love*

LEAH DOBRINSKA

Copyright © 2023 by Leah Dobrinska

All rights reserved.

No portion of this book may be reproduced in any form without written permission from the publisher or author, except in the case of brief quotations embodied in critical articles or reviews.

In accordance with the U.S. Copyright Act of 1976, the scanning, uploading, and electronic sharing of any part of this book without the permission of the author is unlawful piracy and theft of the author's intellectual property. Thank you for your support of the author's rights.

This book is entirely a work of fiction. Names, characters and incidents portrayed in it are either the work of the author's imagination or are used fictitiously. Any resemblance to actual persons, living or dead, businesses, companies, events or localities is entirely coincidental.

Cover Design: Ana Grigoriu-Voicu with Books-design

Author Photo: Beth Dunphy

ISBN: 978-1-7374483-6-5 (paperback) | 978-1-7374483-7-2 (ebook)

For Nick. Always.

Chapter 1

KRISTY

KRISTY VOS WAS IN complete control of the situation...just how she liked it. She was doing her best impression of Jennifer Lopez in her iconic role in *The Wedding Planner* (brown M&Ms *forever*), albeit, minus the headset.

Though if she could have pulled off a headset with her bridesmaid dress, she totally would have.

As it was, she took up her place at the back of Our Lady of Good Hope Church with a happy heart. Her cousin's New Year's Eve wedding ceremony had gone seamlessly. Gidget and John, the blissful newlyweds, were now greeting guests in the receiving line, and Kristy was on hand to make sure everything stayed on schedule and to put out any fires.

She had already re-affixed three of the groomsmen's boutonnieres so they were ready for the next round of photos. She'd helped get deodorant lines out of the mother of the groom's black dress. And she'd thwarted a plan set in motion by the precocious flower girl and conniving ring bearer to sneak up into the bell tower and wreak who knows what sort of havoc.

Yep. Everything was under control.

Kristy gripped Gidget's gargantuan bouquet of white roses in one hand and her smaller arrangement in the other as she ran through her mental checklist of what had to happen between the move from church to the park for outdoor photos and then the arrival at the reception hall two hours later.

"Hey, Kristy. We've got a problem."

Kristy turned to see Sarah, one of Gidget's other bridesmaids, striding toward her with an anxious look on her face.

"What's wrong?"

"Mark, John's brother, just told me John couldn't find the key to his truck before the ceremony. His uncle is supposed to drive it to the reception hall so it'll be there for John and Gidget to leave in tonight." Sarah worried her lip.

"No problem. Here. Hold these." Kristy handed off the bouquets. "Gidget has John's spare key on her key ring, and her keys are in the side pocket of my purse for safe keeping. Let me head to the bride's room and grab them."

Sarah's shoulders relaxed. "Oh, thank goodness."

Kristy nodded, shooting her a reassuring smile. "I'll be right back. Stay here in case Gidget needs anything while I'm gone."

She took off in the opposite direction with purpose and complete composure, her high heels clicking on the tile floor in the church's narthex. She waved and smiled at the familiar faces of friends and family members mingling in cheerful groups around the back of the church.

As soon as Kristy turned the corner down the hall that led to the bride's room, she hiked up the long trail of emerald chiffon from where it was swishing around her ankles and picked up her pace only to come to a complete and unexpected halt when she ran smack into a titanic wall of muscle.

Kristy teetered on her heels, nearly losing her balance, until a pair of large, warm hands grasped her around her waist.

"I'm so sorry, I wasn't—" Her excuse died on her lips as she looked up into the ocean blue eyes of Ashton Klink.

"Hi." Ashton stared down at her. A smile tugged at his lips, giving his angular features a trace of velvety softness.

"Ashton?" Kristy squeaked out his name.

She tried to regain her composure, but his hands were still touching her hips, and every single other thought fled from her mind as if being chased out by a raging, Ashton-shaped bull.

His sandy blonde hair was cut short on the sides and folded over at a neat part. It was gelled, but it didn't look like he was trying too hard. His midnight blue suit fit him to perfection, stretching tautly across shoulders that seemed to go on for days. The cords of his neck—a feature she had never paid any attention to on anyone before this very instant—were smooth and firm, a teasing glimpse at what she imagined were the strong lines of the rest of his sculpted body.

Some things never changed, and Ashton Klink's good looks were one of them.

He was also still her brother's best friend.

So there was that.

But Ashton was staring at her like he never had before. The intense desire glimmering in his eyes made her feel at once deeply confident and, at the same time, utterly exposed.

Growing up, he'd never really given her the time of day. He'd always been nice, but she was Vince's little sister to him—at least that's how it seemed. That hadn't stopped her from secretly pining over him all through high school, when she'd thought Ashton Klink was what goals and dreams were made of.

Now, she wasn't sure what to think or what to do.

Kristy gulped and took a step back, brushing down the front of her dress. "I-I didn't expect to see you here."

Ashton rocked on his heels, clasping his hands easily behind his back. "I wasn't sure I would make it, but the timing of my leave worked out. I called John earlier this week, and he said to come."

Kristy nodded. From what she'd gathered from Vince over the years, Ashton commissioned into the Marine Corps after graduating from college. As far as she knew, he hadn't been back to Mapleton, Wisconsin, their shared home town, since.

She pasted on what she hoped was a friendly smile and made herself think about wedding-related things. Anything to prevent her from focusing on how her heart was playing a persistent percussion in her chest, the beat getting louder in her ears with each second he held her gaze. "Well, that's great. I'll adjust the seating chart and get you a place card as soon as we get over to the reception hall."

Ashton arched an eyebrow. "Uh, okay. I hope it's not too much trouble."

Kristy shook her head quickly. "Not at all. I'm in charge of making sure things go off without a hitch here, so I'll get you taken care of."

A rush of both hot and cold flooded her body the second the words—accidentally dripping with double meaning—left her mouth.

Ashton pressed his lips together, as if trying to hide a smile. "Thanks for that."

"Right." Kristy ducked her chin but not before she caught sight of the way his eyes flickered with good humor.

She could drown in those eyes, and what a way to go.

Kristy sucked in a breath. She was being ridiculous, and she needed to get out of his presence before she made any more of a fool out of herself. "If you'll excuse me, I have to go find something for the bride and groom."

Ashton stepped to the side and swept his arm in front of his impressive frame, giving her a half bow. "By all means, don't let me stop you."

"Thanks." She chuckled in spite of herself, Ashton's theatrics somehow putting her at ease.

With one last glance in his direction, she scooped up the layers of her dress again and hurried down the hall, leaving him standing behind her.

She could feel him staring at her back. Knowing he was watching her sent the hairs along her arms ratcheting to attention, as if she'd been shocked by some sort of starry-eyed power source.

"Hey, Kristy."

She froze at the sound of his deep, searing voice saying her name. She spun around. "Yeah?"

"It's really good to see you." He flashed a warm, sincere smile that somehow perfectly filled the width between the chiseled right angles of his jaw.

Kristy swallowed a couple of times, but it felt like cotton balls were lining the ridges of her esophagus. Why couldn't she speak when he was looking at her?

Probably because he was looking at her like *that*. And after everything that happened with Declan, she didn't know if a man would ever look at her like *that* again.

She gave herself a mental shake. She was not going to focus on past heartache today. In fact, she could barely remember what Declan looked like—not in the wake of her run-in with Ashton, anyway.

Kristy smiled back at him, willing her voice to come out sounding relaxed and unaffected. "You too, Ashton."

They stared at each other for a second longer before Kristy turned away, forcing her attention to the task at hand. She had a job to do and a to-do list a mile long. She didn't have time to overanalyze Ashton's intentions.

Or to dwell on the fact that when he smiled at her—*her*—his face was filled with enough light to put the winter sun to shame.

·♥·♥·♥·♥·♥·

ASHTON

Ashton sat at the back of Heritage Hall on a cushioned barstool, nursing a glass of whiskey. The lights were dimmed and the dance floor was packed in front of him. Gidget and John's family and friends shimmied around with limbs flying this way and that, celebrating the couple's marriage.

Ashton's eyes flitted across the room. He saw familiar faces in every corner.

It was weird to be back in Mapleton. Weird, but good.

As if pulled by some sort of invisible string, Ashton's gaze landed on Kristy. He blew out a shaky breath.

She was mesmerizing, and she had no idea.

Ashton was man enough to admit he was staring. Truth be told, he'd been staring for most of the day—all throughout the ceremony and then again in the church's hallway. He couldn't help it. At the sight of her in that evergreen dress, with its figure-fitting beaded top and flowy, feminine skirt, Ashton's world had tipped on its axis, and everything slid straight in the direction of Kristy.

And that was before she'd turned her smile on him.

Now, he watched her bare feet peek out from underneath the gown as she fluttered around the hall, stopping to chat with wedding attendees at a table near the front of the room. She turned and waved over one of the hall's employees, pointing him in the direction of the kitchen. A couple minutes later the man returned with a fresh glass of champagne. Kristy delivered it to someone at the table before bending down and receiving a hug.

Ashton's fingers twitched, longing to touch her. What would it feel like to hold her close to him? To hold the attention of those bright, brown eyes?

He'd gotten a taste earlier today, and he craved more.

Ashton groaned and took another drink of his whiskey.

When he'd decided to come back to Mapleton, he had no intention of getting hung up on his childhood crush.

But being in Kristy's presence was like being sucked into the middle of a funnel cloud. Not only was he physically attracted to her, but he'd always been drawn to the way she commanded a room.

Growing up, they were opposites in that way. Where Ashton was quiet and reserved, Kristy was bold and full of energy.

He'd considered her off limits as his best friend's little sister, so he'd never really gotten to know her. But that didn't mean he didn't respect and admire her from a distance.

And boy, did he want to get to know the woman she'd grown into now.

"Ashton, dear, how wonderful to see you again."

He blinked and tore his eyes from Kristy, turning his attention to the older woman who'd joined him at the bar, his former neighbor, Nancy Hollace.

She stood at his side, staring up at him with a wide smile on her wrinkled face.

He bent to kiss her papery cheek. "You too, Mrs. Hollace. You look as lovely as ever."

"Hush." Nancy swatted his arm, but her eyes danced with pleasure. "You always were such a good boy. I'm so glad you could make it."

"Me too. My schedule fell into place, and here I am."

"Well, I sure am happy about that. I know your folks are no longer village residents, but that doesn't mean we don't still claim you as our own, you hear?"

Ashton nodded, rubbing his brow to cover his wince at the mention of his mom and dad. His parents' messy divorce had been front-page news in the small Village of Mapleton. He dreaded the sorry stares and gossip of well-meaning neighbors. He'd had enough of that to last a lifetime the summer before he went off to college, and that was the main reason he hadn't returned to Mapleton in the past several years. He didn't love reliving that time in his life. He'd put it behind him and paved his own way.

Fortunately, Nancy—who'd always been a grandmother figure to him—didn't seem to want to dredge up the past, nor was she looking at him with pity. Instead, she looked proud. He loved her for that.

"Still with the Marines out in North Carolina?" When he nodded, Nancy pressed him for more information. "How long are you in town for?"

"Just the week. I'm crashing at Vince's house until I have to get back to base."

Nancy bobbed her head up and down, peering at him as if she could see into his soul. "Anyone in particular you're getting back to out there?"

That was the other thing about Mapleton. He'd almost forgotten how people here made everyone's personal lives their own business. He could hardly hold that against sweet, old Nancy. An indulgent smile worked its way onto his face. "No, ma'am."

Nancy harrumphed. "Well, you enjoy a little down time. Who knows? Maybe you'll meet someone here." She shifted her attention to the dance floor, tipping her chin in a particular direction.

Ashton tracked her stare and was startled to see Kristy again. He rolled his head back down to Nancy who was looking up at him with a knowing grin.

"Very well, then. I'll let you enjoy the rest of your night." With that, she turned to leave, her billowy shawl flapping in her wake. He stared after her, and she swung her head around, glancing at him over her shoulder. "You stay in touch now, dear. We're always praying for you."

"Thanks, Mrs. Hollace." Ashton's insides warmed with more than just whiskey at the thought that no matter where the Marine Corps sent him, Nancy Hollace in Mapleton would be offering up Hail Marys for his safety. It was nice to feel looked after.

As Nancy floated off, Ashton's interest returned to the dance floor.

To Kristy.

She and Vince had started some sort of dance to *Who Let the Dogs Out*. They were crawling around on the floor on all fours, like dogs, alternatingly lifting their legs as if next to a fire hydrant. A smile pulled at his lips as he watched Kristy really get into it. Soon, the whole dance floor was joining in.

And that, he thought, summed up his best friend's sister.

She was the heartbeat of the party.

The music changed to Elvis Presley crooning about wise men and fools rushing in, and the dancers coupled off. Ashton glanced down at his watch. It was eleven thirty on New Year's Eve.

When he looked back up, Kristy had wandered over to the nearest side of the dance floor and was watching the couples spinning around.

He downed the rest of his drink and screwed up his courage, sliding off his chair and walking toward her.

Reaching her side, he cleared his throat.

She turned and looked up at him, her hazelnut eyes flaring. "Ashton! Hi."

He held out his hand. "Would you like to dance?"

She stared at his open palm for what felt like an eternity, before placing her much smaller hand in his. "Sure."

Ashton led her to an open spot along the periphery of dancers and drew her close to his chest, letting his hands rest around her trim waist.

She tentatively lifted her arms up and placed them on his shoulders. Her uncharacteristic shyness had his mouth going dry.

"So." He hadn't thought much past this point, and now that he'd gotten her here, in his arms, he realized he should probably say something to her—try to be charming or witty. But he was so dumbstruck by her face and the feel of her soft curves molding against him, he couldn't seem to generate a topic for conversation.

Kristy looked up at him through her eyelashes. "Are you having a nice time?"

Ashton nodded, grateful to her for rescuing him from his tongue-tied self. "I am. It's really nice to see everyone, and the wedding was beautiful."

Kristy sighed, a dreamy smile drifting across her face. "It really was, wasn't it?"

"You did a good job."

"I was prepared. Even my lists had lists." She chuckled in a way that was endearingly self-deprecating. "Some may say I'm a control freak, but as a result, everything went smoothly. I just wanted it to be a perfect day for Gidget and John."

"I'm sure they're very grateful." Ashton marveled at Kristy's selfless heart. She didn't seem to think anything of going above and beyond to put others' needs first. It was incredibly attractive.

He shifted, drawing her a fraction of an inch closer to him as they lapsed into silence. His chin brushed against the top of her hair, and he caught a whiff of vanilla and something fruity. Against his chest, her chest moved up and down with her breath.

She turned her head and looked up at him again. "How long are you in town for?"

Ashton swallowed. "A week, and then I'm leave—"

"Hey, Kristy."

Kristy swiveled around in his arms. Her brother Vince was standing behind her.

Ashton bit back his frustration at the interruption.

Vince shot Ashton a questioning look before turning his attention to Kristy. "Mom sent me to get you. She said Gidget needs your help before the final send off."

Kristy's eyelids fluttered, as if coming back to full consciousness. She nodded. "Right. Of course." She took a step away before stopping and offering him a small smile. "Thanks for the dance."

"Anytime." He smiled back at her, wanting to say so much more, but not, he thought, in the presence of Vince or in the middle of the dance floor.

Unfortunately, he didn't know if he'd get another chance.

And on that sobering note, Ashton decided to call it a night.

Chapter 2

Kristy

Kristy stumbled down the stairs at Vince's house on New Year's Day, the hundred-year old steps groaning under her feet. She'd gone to bed with her contact lenses in and now her eyes felt like they were filled with super glue. She blinked a couple of times, gripping the rail and trying to make as little noise as possible on her way to her brother's kitchen.

She needed coffee.

Copious amounts of coffee.

The morning sun shone through Vince's kitchen window and cast harsh shadows across the space as she shuffled to open the cabinet to the right of the sink. Retrieving one of her brother's gazillion mugs (a byproduct of being a school teacher), she rifled around the lazy Susan looking for Vince's canister of coffee grounds. Finally, she put her hands on it and stood up to get a pot brewing.

The floor creaked behind her, and Kristy whirled around. Her hand connected with the coffee mug on the counter, sending it toppling into the sink with a resounding clatter.

"Ashton?" Kristy pressed her palm to her chest. "What are you doing here?" She willed her heart rate to get into line so her next words would come out sounding less breathless.

Ashton leaned on the arm of Vince's couch with his long legs extended out straight, looking far too awake and put together for eight o'clock on New Year's morning. In a blink, he'd taken her in, his gaze sweeping from head to toe before settling back on her face.

Kristy glanced down at the baggy sweatshirt and oversized flannel pants she'd found in her brother's spare closet last night. She hadn't bothered to wash her face, so the previous day's mascara was clumping to her eyelashes. She put a hand to where her up-do from the wedding was still holding on by a bobby-pin thread. The hairspray was hard to the touch, and her entire head felt lopsided.

Her whole body heated under his stare.

"Good morning to you, too, Kristy." Ashton's deep voice rolled over her like an avalanche, but instead of cooling her down, the sound of it may as well have thrown a gallon of gasoline on the fire.

He folded his arms and raised his massive shoulders in a small shrug. "And to answer your question, I'm staying with Vince this week. Didn't he tell you?"

"No. He didn't." Kristy turned to start the coffee. She frantically shoved a flyaway strand of hair behind her ear, but she was pretty sure it wasn't going to help her cause. Maybe if she just owned the fact that she looked like she'd been run over by a truck, it would make it all a little less embarrassing. "Gosh, I'm a mess."

"You're not a mess."

Kristy peeked over her shoulder to see Ashton staring at her again. She was sure he was just saying that to make her feel better, but he sounded earnest and his gaze was as intense as it had been yesterday at church.

Like maybe he liked what he saw.

She pushed the thought away. This was Ashton Klink she was talking about. He didn't see her like that. He couldn't.

Could he?

Her nervous energy came out in a self-effacing laugh. "Thanks for saying so, but I am. I only asked if I could sleep here late last night. I didn't want to drive back to my place in Apple Creek after we got done cleaning up the reception hall. But I didn't come prepared. Clearly." She widened her stance and motioned to her attire.

Ashton stole another full-body look before catching her eye. "I think you look great."

She giggled because she didn't know what else to do. She didn't know how to be on the receiving end of his attention. Certainly not now, in her current state. And really, not ever.

She pointed at him. "You're one to talk."

He arched a brow.

"I mean, look at yourself." She wiggled her finger around in a circle.

He looked down and then back at her, an amused smirk giving his dangerously handsome face an added air of charm. "You think I look good?"

She rolled her eyes, the tips of her ears sizzling. "As if you don't already know."

He chuckled. "Nah. It's nice to hear you say it, though."

Kristy thought she might spontaneously combust. Was she flirting with Ashton Klink? Was *he* flirting with *her*? And why did it feel so easy?

Her high school self would have died if she could see her now.

Kristy swallowed. "So, you're up early."

Ashton rumbled out another low chuckle, and even as she was sweating under layers of flannel and cotton, goosebumps paraded up and down Kristy's arms.

"A byproduct of the job, I suppose."

"Right. Military life. O'Dark Thirty and all that." She clicked her tongue. "Probably accounts for the muscles, too."

Kristy sucked in a breath. Had she said that out loud?

Ashton shot her a smoldering look and then he winked.

He actually winked.

And somehow made it look good.

"I guess so." He unfolded his large, muscle-packed frame and stood up from the edge of the couch. He walked toward where she was still standing, swimming in her brother's clothes, in the kitchen.

"How's all that going by the way? Military life, I mean." Kristy's pulse spiked to a dangerous level as he came closer to her. She spun to face the sink and hide the fact that he was having such an effect on her. She turned on the tap and filled a glass.

"It's good. I like what I do. I think I'm good at it."

"I'm sure you're wonderful at it." She took a sip of water, getting a hold of herself. She had been in the presence of other attractive men, after all. She could take part in a pleasant conversation with Ashton. She pivoted, held her ground, and smiled up at him...hoping to present herself as confident and capable.

But when he stepped directly in front of her, her knees liquefied. She had to grip the counter to keep her balance.

"Thank you." Ashton's tone was sincere as he brushed past her, reaching around to retrieve his own coffee mug. Kristy caught a whiff of cinnamon coming off of his skin. It was unfair that in her current state, he managed to both look and smell so good, but she could hardly complain. She took a deep breath, trying to memorize the scent before telling herself to knock it off. She wasn't a bloodhound.

He eased back, leaning against the peninsula and giving her a little more breathing room. Not much, but a little.

"Mind if I have a cup?"

Kristy nodded as the pot behind her gurgled and finished brewing. "Of course. I made plenty."

She filled each of their mugs, and they sipped in silence for a minute. "So, any big plans for the new year?"

Ashton paused with his mug to his mouth before slowly lowering it, his eyes on her as he answered. "Well, I'll spend most of it on a ship in the middle of the Mediterranean Sea."

Kristy choked on her coffee, sputtering out a mouthful of the hot liquid and spitting it into the sink. She wiped her mouth with the back of her hand, eyes watering as she gaped at him. "You're deploying?"

♥ · ♥ · ♥ · ♥ · ♥

ASHTON

"Yeah. Middle of this month." Ashton took another sip of his coffee, watching Kristy the whole time.

She looked adorable this morning, all woozily and sleep-deprived. If he'd been captivated by her put-together appearance at the wedding yesterday, then seeing her like this—so unassuming and real—was enough to bring him to his knees.

When she staggered into the kitchen, he had gulped and immediately started going through military history statics in his head so as not to focus on the fact that he'd woken up in the same house as Kristy.

It felt peculiarly intimate.

Now here he was having coffee with her.

He waited in silence while she digested the news of his deployment.

Eventually, she turned her wide-eyed gaze at him. "I had no idea."

Her voice was quieter than it had been. He wasn't sure what to make of it.

"I thought maybe Vince told you."

Kristy gave her head a rueful shake. "Again, nope. I'm going to need to have a word with him about filling me in on things where you're concerned."

Her comment made Ashton smile even though she probably didn't mean much by it. But the thought that Kristy would care to know anything about him sent a swoop of pleasure through his stomach.

She motioned to the living room. "Should we sit?"

He nodded and followed her to the couch.

She sat on one end and tucked her legs up underneath her. He sat on the other side, leaving a full cushion between them.

She blew into her mug, looking at him over the rim. "So bring me up to speed. Is this your first deployment?"

He leaned into the couch, crossing his legs in front of him. "I deployed to do earthquake relief work in Haiti a couple years back. And I've been sent different places stateside for a month or two here and there, but this will be the first time I head overseas."

Kristy raised her eyebrows. "Wow. You're so calm about it all. Are you excited to go?"

Ashton rubbed his hand against the back of his neck. "I wouldn't say excited, no. But it's a part of the job. When the Marine Corps says *go here* or *do that*, I do as instructed."

Kristy hunched her shoulders over her coffee cup and shuddered. "I cannot imagine not having control over my schedule, and being at the disposal of...who makes the decisions? The President?"

Ashton chuckled. "He's the Commander in Chief. But he's not my immediate boss."

"I figured as much." Kristy shrugged, taking a drink of her coffee. "But you like what you do, then? You don't mind the uncertainty of all of it?"

Ashton cocked his head to the side, weighing his answer. "I do like it. For now. I love the people I get to work with. I like making a difference. And getting to see the world is a perk. But I don't know how sustainable the lifestyle is. Once I have a wife, she'll obviously have a say. It's hard to imagine leaving a family behind. In the future, I mean."

The word 'wife' seemed to carry with it extra meaning, and it hung in the air between them for what felt like ages, giving the room an unmistakable charge. He hadn't meant to heighten the intimacy of the moment, but he definitely had.

Was Kristy picturing herself as his wife? Because for some reason, he was.

Ashton took a gulp of coffee, wishing the couch would swallow him up. *What* had gotten into him?

Kristy batted her eyes a couple of times. "Right. Of course. That makes sense. So, no girlfriend that you're leaving behind then?"

Kristy's blatant inquiry into his personal life made him feel marginally better. Ashton fought a smile. "Nope. Not for me. Not for a while, actually. What about you?"

She shook her head. "No one special. There was a guy I dated during law school, but it didn't work out. We broke up over a year ago."

"I see." Ashton stared into his coffee, wondering who in their right mind would break up with Kristy.

She shifted her legs, causing the couch cushions to dip.

He glanced over in time to catch her smiling at him. She didn't look away, and the floppy, baggy fit of her sweatshirt somehow added to her allure. "Well, I'm glad you're here. Even if it's just for a little while."

Ashton's heart rate took off faster than an F-16 fighter jet at the sight of the sweetest, most genuine look in her deep-set eyes.

In that moment, there was nowhere else he'd rather be.

He took a drink to try to open up his throat, but his voice still came out sounding gravely. "Me too."

They stared at each other, and Ashton swore a jolt of electricity arced across the couch. Kristy's cheeks flushed, and her mouth parted half an inch, so he was pretty sure she felt it, too.

"What in the name of all that is good are you two doing up so early?" Vince stomped into the living room and shot an annoyed glare in their direction. "It's a vacation day—my *last* vacation day before school starts up again, if you didn't recall. I'm letting you both crash here. The least you could do if you were going to be awake is keep it down. All sorts of clanging in the kitchen and this constant chatter is not helpful for my beauty sleep."

The spell between them snapped at Vince's entrance.

Across the couch from him, Kristy rolled her eyes. "You'd need to sleep for a year to fix that face of yours."

Ashton grinned into his coffee. He always loved how the brother-sister relationship between Vince and Kristy played out. They teased each other, but they also always had each other's back.

Vince joined them in the living room, plopping down in the middle of the couch and rubbing his knuckles over the top of Kristy's head. "Hasn't anyone informed you we look alike, sis?"

"Vince, cut it out!" she shrieked.

Vince smirked and turned to Ashton. "So, what's the plan for today? Do you still want to work out?"

"If possible, that would be great."

A major perk of Vince's job as teacher and high school football coach was his access to the weight room during off hours.

Vince swung around to face Kristy. "Want to come with us up to the high school?"

"Sure." Kristy downed the rest of her coffee. "I could use a run. I've got my workout clothes in my car." She hopped off the couch and crossed in front of them, heading for the kitchen.

Ashton tried not to stare at the smooth curve of her neck. Given her current outfit, it was the only skin exposed. He wondered what it would feel like to be the one who got to trail kisses along her neck and the delicate line of her jaw.

Vince slapped Ashton on the back, smacking some sense into him, before he stood up.

"Alright. If we're awake, we may as well do something useful. Car's leaving in ten minutes. Hop to it."

"You would have made a great drill sergeant, you know that?" Ashton deadpanned.

Kristy giggled, shaking her head at the two of them before she went outside, presumably to fetch her things.

Ashton's heart lurched. He wanted her to come back so he could try to make her laugh again.

Instead, he was left with Vince, who pointed at him.

"Someone's got to keep you in line."

Vince disappeared up the stairs, leaving Ashton to his thoughts.

If Vince only knew...

Ashton set down his coffee mug and scrubbed his hands over his face.

What was he doing? He was leaving the country in less than three weeks, and Kristy had just told him she couldn't imagine dealing with the uncertainty of military life.

No matter how drawn to her he was—no matter how much he admired her—he had no business getting tied up with his best friend's sister.

Not now. And probably not ever.

The only issue? He didn't know if he could help himself.

Chapter 3

KRISTY

No one should look *that good in a t-shirt.*

Kristy stepped up onto the treadmill and set the tempo for her run, marveling at the scene in front of her.

The Mapleton High School weight lifting complex was relatively new. The free weights, benches, and squatting racks were positioned on the lower level, and the bikes, treadmills, and other machines were a story above, on a balcony overlooking the weight room.

As a result, Kristy had a bird's-eye view of her brother and Ashton as they went through their workout.

Let's be real. She couldn't care less about her brother at the moment. Her eyes were glued to Ashton. He'd changed from the white t-shirt he wore for coffee this morning to an olive green one. She didn't think it was possible, but the new shirt somehow further accentuated the muscles of his upper body. He was shaped like a perfect upside down triangle—broad, chiseled shoulders tapering to a narrow waist.

And while she couldn't deny her attraction to his outward appearance, she found herself just as attracted to his heart. The pure sweetness of his comment about how his wife would obviously have a say in his future career had made her stomach bottom out.

Yep, Ashton was steady and solid all the way around. She had no doubt he was the type of leader all those Marine Corps commercials—the ones with the dragon and the mountain and the sword—attested to. He was one of the few and the proud.

Even though she didn't have any claim to him, she was proud of him. But she was feeling something else toward him, too. Beyond her attraction. Beyond her pride. There was something she couldn't quite put her finger on. As she circled around it, she realized she was anxious.

Worried for his safety.

Worried that she was finally getting a chance to get to know him only for him to be leaving not just the town, but the country.

Worried because she wanted to be able to control what was happening and she couldn't.

Kristy filled her cheeks with air and released it on a hiss. Her thoughts were spinning out of control.

She cranked up the Taylor Swift song that was blasting through her headphones, and forced her mind to go blank. She always loved running because it helped her clear her head, and if there was ever a day where she needed some clarity, it was today.

She stretched out her stride, working out the sore muscles from the hours in heels yesterday and letting her body move in time to the music, until the shrill ringing of her phone cut off the song.

Kristy glanced down to where she had her phone wedged in the cup holder.

She pressed the button to answer. "Hi, Mom."

"Goodness, Kristy. You're panting. Did I catch you at a bad time?"

Kristy snorted and reached down to grab the hem of her t-shirt, using it to wipe her brow. "I'm running."

"Well, aren't you ambitious the morning after the wedding? Starting the new year off on the right foot literally, eh?" Her mom, Paige, laughed at her own joke.

Kristy coughed, laboring over her words as she tried to keep up her pace. "I tagged along with Vince and Ashton. We're at the high school."

"Oh how nice!" Her mom's tone oozed with pleasure. "How is Ashton? I didn't get a chance to chat with him much yesterday."

"He's good. He's deploying in a few weeks."

"I had heard that."

Kristy drew in a ragged breath, focusing on her stride. Did everyone know he was leaving except for her? Something about that made her belly twist into a knot. "I didn't know."

"Yes, I think Vince told me. I don't remember now. I must've forgotten to mention it to you. I'm sorry about that. Are you okay with it?"

Kristy swallowed the stickiness in her mouth. "Why wouldn't I be? I have no claim over Ashton. It's not like I really have a say in where the military sends him."

"Well of course not, but you've always had a soft spot for that boy. I don't imagine it's easy to think about him out there in harm's way. How long is he staying in Mapleton?"

That was so like her mom—reading her like a book and then shifting the conversation without giving Kristy a chance to confirm or deny her assessment. In this case, Kristy was grateful not to dwell on her crush. Here she thought she'd been so discreet in high school, keeping her feelings for Ashton a secret. She had no clue her mom had been on to her.

"He said he's here for a week."

"How nice. You bring him to family dinner tonight, alright?"

Kristy groaned. "Mom, I'm sure he has other things to do."

"Other things like what, dear? He doesn't have family around anymore. We're practically his family. Why don't you let him say yes or no. Just ask him for me."

"Fine." Kristy exhaled. "I'm going to go here." She licked her lips as below her Ashton and Vince moved from doing sets of curls with the dumbbells to the bench press.

"Yes, I'll let you get back to it. Maybe snap a picture."

Kristy stutter stepped. "I'm sorry, what?"

Paige's light laugh tinkled over the phone. "If the man looks half as good working out as he did last night in his suit, then I'd get some photo evidence if I were you. You know, to save for a rainy day."

"Oh my gosh, Mom. You're ridiculous." Thank goodness no one could hear this conversation. Her mom could be so embarrassing.

And also not half wrong.

"Don't tell me you weren't just thinking the exact same thing."

Busted.

Kristy zoned in on Ashton's biceps as Vince stood at his head and spotted him while he lifted an obscene amount of weight. She tried to do the quick math of the plates on the bar, but the numbers got jumbled in her head as she watched his forearms flex with each extension. A small tattoo peeked out from under his shirt sleeve, and wow, it was suddenly all she could think about.

"That's what I thought."

Her mom's teasing voice in her ear made her trip.

Kristy grabbed the bars on either side of the treadmill to steady herself. "I'm not making any promises, Mom."

"Just do your best with the picture. And be sure to invite him to dinner! I'll see you tonight."

Her phone beeped, and Kristy looked down at the display screen to see her mom had disconnected the call.

Okay, then.

·❤·❤·❤·❤·❤·

ASHTON

"Dude, you're making me look bad." Vince peered down at Ashton from where he stood spotting his bench press.

Ashton grunted, shoving the weight back up on an exhale. "In front of who, your sister? I doubt she's paying us any attention."

Vince scoffed. "Well, yeah. But on the off chance she looks down here, I'd like her to still think of me as half-way strong, which she won't do now that you're in here showing me up."

Ashton racked the bar and sat up on the bench, casting a quick look up to where Kristy was running.

He caught her eye, and she shot him a smile before staring straight ahead again, her legs churning at an impressive pace.

Ashton waved, feeling like a lovesick teenager. Maybe it was being back in his high school. Or maybe it was just being around Kristy again. "She's still quite a runner, huh?"

Vince nodded. "She's training for her first half marathon. She says running is her therapy. Helps her clear her head."

"Is her job pretty stressful, then?" Ashton wanted to know everything about her life. The good and the bad. What made her tick. There was so much he was in the dark about.

"You'd have to ask her."

"I might do that." Ashton reached for the water bottle at his feet while he lobbed out a verbal grenade. "She told me she wasn't dating anyone."

"Not at the moment. Or not that I know of, anyway. Why? Are you interested?" Vince stepped up alongside of him, waiting as he chugged water.

Ashton didn't make it a habit of beating around the bush, and Vince was his best friend. He would shoot straight with him, even if it was awkward. He swallowed and met Vince's gaze, shrugging. "How would you feel if I was?"

Vince frowned. "I don't know, sort of weird." He stared hard at Ashton before looking up and over his shoulder to where Kristy was running. "She's an adult, though. So are you."

Ashton let out a breath. As far as blessings went, it wasn't much—not that he was really looking for one. He didn't know what he was looking for, but the more he thought about Kristy, the more he wanted to pursue her. And he may as well be honest about it.

"I'm still sorting through everything, and I don't know..." Ashton trailed off. "Don't tell her I said anything, okay?"

Vince pinned him with a stern, protective big-brother look. "Just don't mess with her, man. She's had enough where that came from, and she doesn't need it from you."

Ashton held up his hands in defense, his heart hammering at the thought of someone hurting Kristy. "I would never do that."

"I know you wouldn't try to, but..." Vince shrugged and turned back to the bar, slipping a forty five pound weight off one side.

Ashton stood and started helping Vince with the re-rack, lost in his own thoughts.

The only way he could know for sure he wouldn't hurt Kristy was to keep his distance, but he didn't know if he could do that.

Not after seeing her again after all these years and having such a powerful reaction to her.

And after this morning, he had to think the feelings weren't one-sided.

Would he be able to live with himself if he didn't take a chance on seeing where something with Kristy could go? Even if it was the worst timing in the world?

Vince lay down on the bench and started pressing, and Ashton stepped up to spot him.

"Hey, you two." Kristy appeared at Ashton's side, and his synapses went from zero to sixty, firing in overdrive. She looked over the bar and wagged her eyebrows. "Looking good, big bro."

Vince grunted. "Gotta keep my muscles up so I can protect my baby sister."

Kristy rolled her eyes. "I'm perfectly capable of protecting myself, Vince."

Vince finished his last rep and racked the bar with a clank. "Yeah, yeah." He shot Ashton a look.

Kristy stared between them, and her eyebrows rose. She wiped at the bead of sweat trickling down her temple.

Ashton shook his head at his friend. Vince was about as subtle as a freight train barreling through town in the dead of night.

"Anyway, our mom called." She pointed at herself and then at Vince before swinging her full attention to Ashton. "You've been summoned to family dinner tonight." She grimaced. "I don't think she's going to take no for an answer. Can you come?"

Ashton smiled. "I'd love to. I didn't get much of a chance to connect with your mom yesterday. It'll be good to see her."

Kristy looked relieved. "That's what she said, too. She's expecting us all at six."

Vince rubbed his hands together. "She told me she's making her famous lasagna."

Ashton's mouth began to water. "Well if I wasn't sold at the mere thought of spending time with you fine people, that would have done it. I would sell my right arm for a slice of your mom's lasagna."

"You and me both, my man." Vince reached up his hand for a high five, and Ashton slapped it, grateful things were normal between them.

Kristy chuckled. "You guys are weird. Do you have much longer?"

Vince answered for them both. "Just have to cool down and stretch."

Kristy nodded and wandered off to the side of the weight room, clicking around on her phone.

Ashton helped Vince put the weights away. When he turned toward Kristy, she had her phone up but she dropped it quickly to her side, a *caught-with-one-hand-in-the-cookie-jar* look casting an intriguing mix of guilt and pleasure over her already stunning face. She flashed him a toe-curling smile before turning away.

Whatever that was all about, she sure was cute.

And thanks to Mrs. Vos, he now had a dinner date with the woman he couldn't get out of his head—the one who was quickly filling the place he realized might always have been reserved for her in his heart.

Chapter 4

KRISTY

"YOU JOINING THE NEIGHBORHOOD watch?"

At the taunting lit of Vince's voice, Kristy dropped the edge of the curtain in their mom's living room and jumped away from the window.

Her heart raced, and she'd bet her cheeks matched the dark red upholstery of the couch. "Hasn't anyone ever told you it's not nice to sneak up on people? You scared me half to death."

Vince just laughed. "Not you, too?"

"I—" Kristy frowned. "Wait, what?"

"You've got it bad."

"I do not." Kristy's hands went to her hips. She was naturally argumentative. It came in handy as a lawyer. "Hold on. What do I have bad? And who else has it bad?"

"Never mind. Just a hunch. I'm sure it'll all be very clear in the not so distant future." Vince cocked his head at the sound of an engine pulling into the driveway. "Like right now," he added.

Vince ambled over to the front door and swung it open, waiting for Ashton to make his way up the walk.

Kristy darted into the kitchen, where her mom was pulling a piping hot pan of lasagna out of the oven.

"Oh, good. Can you get a pot holder out of the drawer for me, dear?"

Kristy did as she was asked and set it down on the table, all set and ready for dinner.

"Is he here, yet?"

"Kristy was the first to know." Vince led Ashton into the kitchen. "She was staked out at the window. Like a watch dog."

"Vince!" Kristy couldn't help but sigh. Her brother would be the death of her.

Ashton just chuckled and crossed the room. He wrapped her mom in a giant bear hug. "Mrs. Vos, it's good to see you. Sorry I missed you at the wedding."

Kristy took a beat to study the way the muscles in Ashton's upper arms looked particularly good in the tight fabric of his button up flannel shirt, but mostly she was just touched by the sweetness of the gesture. Even more so when he held out a bouquet of gardenias and handed them to her mom.

Paige took the flowers and beamed back at Ashton. "Nonsense. You're here now. And this is a better environment for catching up anyway. You didn't hear it from me, but my Italian cooking is head and shoulders above that of the chef at Heritage Hall."

With a wink, her mom turned to the sink and retrieved a vase from the cabinet. "You kids wash up and take your seats. Everything is ready to go."

Ashton's gaze connected with Kristy's and he smiled. "Hey, there."

"Hey, yourself. Thanks for coming."

"Barf," Vince muttered on his way to the bathroom.

Kristy ignored him. "Can I get you anything to drink?" She shook her head. "Sorry, I guess we don't have to be all formal. Beer and soda are in the fridge in the garage, just like always. Why don't you help yourself?"

Did her voice sound pitchy? What was *wrong* with her? Ashton had been around a lot growing up, so she should be used to his presence. But she wasn't. Not like this. Not with the way he filled the room with warmth and confidence.

And not with the way he was currently looking at her, with that intense but kind gaze of his.

"Sure. What can I grab for you while I'm out there?"

"La Croix would be great."

Ashton made a face.

"What?"

"Nothing. Just, that stuff sort of tastes like feet, doesn't it?"

Kristy laughed, shaking her head. "No it doesn't."

Ashton didn't look convinced.

"You need a refined palate to appreciate it." She stuck her nose in the air before cutting him with a teasing glance. "And you're one to talk. Are you still drinking Mountain Dew these days?"

Ashton arched a brow. "Impressive that you remember my drink of choice from high school."

"She used to spy on us while we gamed." Vince strolled back into the kitchen.

In the middle of shooting her brother a withering glare, Kristy turned to see Ashton looking earnest.

"Why didn't you say something? You could have played with us."

She smiled at him before he ducked outside to grab drinks. When he reappeared, she said, "Nah. You guys never could have handled me. I'm a Sonic the Hedgehog phenom."

Vince scoffed. "Hardly."

"Do you still have it?" Ashton asked. "The gaming console?"

"In the basement, I think. Why?"

"We should play tonight." Ashton cut her a look. "Make up for some lost time."

Kristy's insides swirled. Was he hinting at what she thought he was hinting at? "I-I'd like that," she said.

"Good. It's a date." The tops of Ashton's cheekbones colored. "Er—you know."

Kristy could not get over how adorable he was. And she was glad to know she wasn't the only one who stuck her foot in her mouth when she got flustered. If anything, his nervousness endeared him to her all the more. There was something about a big, strong man, who was obviously successful and quite capable, being a little shaky when emotions and feelings were on the table.

"Oh brother. You guys are—"

"Ready to eat! I can see that." Her mom bustled toward the table, and Kristy could have kissed her for cutting her brother off before he made another embarrassing comment. Ashton's cheeks were now definitely red, and she'd guess hers matched. Her brother, for his part, seemed to enjoy making them both sweat.

They tucked into a delicious meal.

"I will dream of this lasagna on the ship, Mrs. Vos." Ashton sat back in his seat after finishing his second piece. "Thank you so much for having me."

"You know you're welcome any time. Now." Paige clasped her hands and rested her wrists on the table. "Tell us about what you'll be doing out there. You're a captain now, is that right?"

"Yes, ma'am. Just promoted this past summer. I work as an air traffic control officer, and I'm deploying as part of a MEU."

"A what now?"

"A MEU. Marine Expeditionary Unit. Basically a forward operating air-ground task force. We'll be out in the ocean, ready to go if we're needed."

Kristy's heart dropped into her stomach, and, just as it had this morning when the realities of his career first dawned on her, worry for his safety made saliva pool in the back pockets of her mouth. She shifted in her seat, and she couldn't be sure, but it was as if Ashton picked up on her anxiety.

He looked right at her and added, "The chances of me seeing any sort of active combat are slim. But we're trained and prepared well in any case."

She blew out what she hoped was a discreet breath and offered him a tight smile.

She wanted to look away, to recover her bearing and hide her fear, but Ashton held her gaze, and those eyes of his made her throat go immediately dry.

He opened his mouth to speak again, but Vince asked him a question about whether or not he'd be able to watch the Super Bowl on the ship.

Really, Vince? That's your biggest concern here?

Was she imagining things, or did Ashton seem reluctant to look away from her? A part of her hoped so. A big part of her. She wanted to know what he had been about to say. She wanted to hear everything about his job—to get a handle on it for herself.

Kristy tuned out the guys' follow-up conversation about the chances the Packers had in their upcoming playoff game, instead trying to sort out her thoughts.

She liked Ashton. That's what she kept coming back to. She liked his quiet confidence. The way he commanded attention...and not just because of how he looked. It was how he spoke and how he listened.

The man was something else. He could charm her mom, tease her brother, all while still managing to make her feel like everything she had to say was the most important thing in the world to him.

The whole thing was mind-boggling.

That was half the problem.

Kristy liked to know things, and she knew next to nothing about military life. It made her all sorts of uneasy. Also, he was leaving. And then what would she do?

ASHTON

Ashton was about to lose his fourth Sonic the Hedgehog race. Not for lack of skill. He actually used to be pretty good at the game. But he was so obviously distracted by the woman sitting to his left, the one with determination etched on her sloping brow and a controller clenched between her fingers, that he may as well have forfeited before he even began.

He, Kristy, and Vince had been playing for close to an hour. His stomach muscles hurt from laughing. His mind whirled with the pleasure of talking to Kristy—and Vince, too. It was fun to be around people who knew his history. Who knew where he'd come from, who he was, and who liked him for it all.

For her part, Kristy was hilarious and adorable and charming and smart. In case he'd had any doubts, tonight solidified it for him. His best friend's little sister was the whole package. A couple of times over the course of the evening, he swore she was flirting with him. When their eyes would lock and they'd share a smile. Or when she'd tease him or nudge his shoulder during the game.

If Ashton was being honest, he had already committed the feel of dancing with her—of her in his arms—last night to his memory. After tonight, spending time with her more casually, all he wanted to do was hold her again.

The whooshing sound of Sonic crossing the finish line reached his ears, and he tried to focus on the screen.

Kristy leaned back on the couch and held her arms above her head. The movement sent a tantalizing scent of vanilla wafting in his direction. If only he could figure out a way to liquefy the scent so he could ladle some into a bottle and wear it around his neck, tucked close to his heart.

Dramatic much, man?

"Well, boys. This has been fun. Like I said, Ashton, this is why Vince never let me hang around growing up." She smirked at her brother. "Too embarrassed to be shown up by his baby sister."

Vince scowled at her, and Ashton laughed. "He always was a sore loser."

"Dude. Don't take her side."

"You absolutely can take my side. It's the side of the truth." Kristy dropped her voice and leaned in. Ashton leaned toward her, too. It was as if there was a rushing current flowing from him to her and he was helpless but to get caught up in it. "The side you want to be on."

He couldn't argue with her there.

Their gazes locked, and if Vince wasn't sitting feet from them, Ashton would have leaned the rest of the way in and kissed Kristy...consequences aside.

But Vince was in the room. And it was probably for the best.

Because for all her flirting—for all the fun they'd had—he'd seen the way Kristy stiffened at dinner when he talked about deploying. He didn't want to start something with her if it wasn't what she wanted. He couldn't help but question it all—question if he was just projecting his own desires. Maybe it was wishful thinking to hope that she wanted him the way he wanted her.

Maybe their timing was just off.

As if to solidify the point, Kristy blinked and glanced down into her lap.

"Some of us have to work tomorrow." Vince tossed his controller onto the coffee table and stood up. "You ready, man?"

"Yeah, sure. Of course." He glanced at Kristy, but she still didn't look at him. He wanted to say something. Anything. But he wasn't sure what.

"I'll grab your coat for you." Vince stretched and left the room, heading toward the hall closet.

Ashton stood and held out his hand, praying Kristy would accept it.

When she placed her fingers against his, he swore the electricity he'd felt at the contact last night and again this morning only intensified. He tugged her upright, and she wobbled on her feet, tipping slightly into him.

He reached out his other hand to settle her into place as her palm came to rest on his chest. It worked like a shock paddle, and he felt life course through his veins.

"You okay?" he asked, his voice sounding strangled in his ears.

"Yep. Good. All good." She gazed up at him through her eyelashes.

He was still holding her, and it was not lost on him that she hadn't moved away, nor had she dropped her hand.

Hope sprung up.

Kristy bit her lip, and Ashton swallowed.

His gut was telling him that she wanted him to kiss her. Lord knew *he* wanted to kiss her.

"Kristy." He breathed her name.

"Yeah?"

"Can I—"

"Here ya go."

Kristy took a giant step away from him at Vince's reentry.

Ashton caught the coat his best friend chucked at his head, and he would have liked to strangle him with it. Instead, he slipped his arms into the sleeves, gave Kristy a nod, and followed Vince out the door. What else could he do?

Chapter 5

Kristy

Kristy leaned back in her desk chair and rubbed her temples. The first work day after vacation always seemed to stretch on forever at Mapleton Law, the firm where she practiced. Today was no different.

It didn't help that her head was filled with heart-palpitating, jumbled thoughts of Ashton.

If she wasn't mistaken, he'd almost kissed her last night. She put a finger to her lips. Gosh, she had wanted him to. In the moment, all of her anxieties had fallen away, and her vision had tunneled toward Ashton. All she could think about was how much she enjoyed his company. How he made her feel—intelligent, funny, important.

But of course, Vince had impeccable timing and interrupted whatever was going to happen before it could happen.

And then she started spiraling.

Kristy sighed. She was falling for Ashton, and that scared her. She had a list a mile long of why it was a bad idea.

"Knock, knock."

Kristy glanced up to see Elowen, her paralegal, leaning against the door frame.

Elowen stepped into Kristy's office. "You look deep in thought. Is there anything I can take off your plate?"

Kristy gave her a wry chuckle. "I wish. I'm afraid I'll have to sort this out by myself."

"Is it the Talbit case? That one did look like a doozy when it came across my desk."

Kristy chewed on the inside of her cheek. "No. It's a more personal matter, actually."

Elowen stared at her for a beat before her eyes went as wide as saucers. "Oh my word. You met someone, didn't you?" She took three shuffled steps in her pencil skirt and settled into the guest chair across from Kristy's desk. "Spill."

Kristy clicked her pen open and shut against her chin. "I don't know, El. I don't know what to do. And, it's no one new. He's my brother's best friend."

Elowen gasped and fanned herself. "Oo-la-la."

Kristy rolled her eyes. "I've known him forever."

Elowen sighed. "That's so romantic. Is he cute?"

Kristy reached for her phone and clicked over to the photo her mom had commissioned yesterday. She still couldn't believe she'd gone through with snapping it. Then again, as she stared down at Ashton's hulking figure filling the frame, a corner of his tattoo peeking out from beneath his sleeve in all its tantalizing glory, she toyed with the idea of setting it as her lock screen background. She held up the device facing Elowen.

Her paralegal pressed her lips together. "Okay. He's drop dead gorgeous. Those eyes. Those muscles. Dang, girl." She shot her two thumbs up. "So what's the problem?"

Kristy tossed her phone down onto her desk. "He's a Marine Corps officer."

Elowen blinked. "And?"

"And his life is in North Carolina and mine is here in Wisconsin. And he's deploying in a couple weeks."

Elowen's mouth formed a perfect O. "I see. But you like him, right?"

Kristy nodded. "I do. I always have."

"And he's interested in you?"

Kristy shrugged, a claw of heat working its way up her back at the memory of their near kiss. Still, after Declan, she was wary when it came to discerning what a man felt about her.

"No need to be coy, Kristy. Of course he's interested in you. He'd be crazy not to be."

Kristy shot Elowen an appreciative smile. "Thanks, but I just don't know if it's wise to start something, you know? Not with all the hurdles that will immediately be in our way."

Elowen leaned back in her chair, pressing her fingers together in front of her chest. "I say give it a shot, and don't get too far ahead of yourself. If nothing else, with a guy like him, it'll be a fun week, right? You deserve that." She rose from her seat and brushed down her skirt. "But now if you don't need anything further, I'm heading out for the day."

"Yes, of course, get out of here. And thanks, El."

"Anytime." She clicked her tongue before shooting Kristy a pointed look. "Keep me posted."

Kristy nodded as the door swung shut. She turned over what Elowen had said.

She could have fun. She *wanted* to have fun.

She reached for her phone again, pulling up a group text message and making plans.

The one thing she could control was spending time with Ashton in the here and now, and she didn't want to waste a single minute.

ASHTON

"Come on, man. We're going sledding in the dark."

Ashton glanced up from the book he was reading to see Vince pulling on a pair of sweatpants over his jeans.

"For real?" Ashton slid his bookmark in between the pages of *The Fellowship of the Ring* and stretched his arms over his head. He wasn't used to sitting around all day. He told himself it was good, especially since he was coming into a period of seven to nine months when he'd literally be at work 24/7, but still. He was eager to get out of the house, and he loved sledding. He hadn't been out on a hill in years. The ocean-adjacent location of most Marine Corps bases didn't really provide ample opportunity.

Vince nodded. "Yep. For old time's sake. Kristy coordinated it. Go figure," he added with an affectionate snicker. "A whole group of us are meeting in Sunrise Park. Should be fun."

Ashton was up and off the couch in a flash. He nabbed his phone from the coffee table and checked his messages. He didn't see a text from Kristy, and his shoulders sunk even as he told himself it was ludicrous to feel let down.

"Dude, chill. She texted me and told me to bring you with. She doesn't have your number." Vince shook his head. "You really like her, don't you?"

Ashton offered Vince a sheepish grin. "Am I that obvious?"

Vince grumbled something incoherent, slipping into his winter jacket and stepping into his boots. "Just remember what I said, alright? And, please, I'm begging you, keep the PDA to a minimum around me. I don't know if I can stomach it." He made a gagging face, and chucked a spare pair of boots across the room.

Ashton chuckled, picking up the boots and going to get changed.

His heart strummed with anticipation at the thought of getting close enough to Kristy to have a chance to show her some affection. If he was being honest with himself, he was a little rusty in the relationship department. He'd thrown himself into the job the past few years and that hadn't left much time for a social life.

But this was Kristy. He'd do whatever it took, even if it meant making a blundering fool of himself in the process.

Vince drove them to the sledding hill in Sunrise Park, a sprawling area of woods and trails that also housed the Village of Mapleton's baseball diamonds and soccer fields. They parked in the lot at the bottom of the hill alongside the half-frozen Squirrel River.

It had snowed on and off all day. Now, iridescent, white flakes started falling from the sky, making the night glow brighter, almost hazy. The air smelled clean and fresh, holding with it the promise of a blank-slate future.

Ashton couldn't remember the last time he'd seen snow like this—the kind that clung to tree branches, weighing them down and molding them into crisp, white canopies.

He helped Vince get two plastic sleds, two saucers, and an old-school toboggan out of the bed of his truck before following him to the base of the hill. The group Kristy had compiled was gathered at the top, illuminated by a lone street light positioned along the path beyond the hill. They were a motley crew—dressed in sweatpants, mismatched sweatshirts, and old winter coats. A couple of people had their blaze orange hunting overalls on, and everyone was adorned with scarfs and stocking hats with dangly balls atop, colored in every hue of the rainbow.

Ashton and Vince hiked up the hill. He spotted Kristy the closer they got to the crowd. She wore a bright blue beanie over the top of her dark hair. At the sight of her, the cold, thin, winter air left his lungs.

Vince was right. He really *did* like her.

The second she saw them approaching, a wide smile broke over Kristy's face, and she clomped over to meet them. "You made it!"

She punched her brother in the shoulder before throwing herself into Ashton's arms.

His momentary shock at Kristy's bold behavior turned immediately to pleasure. He wrapped her up, holding her close and savoring the feel of her in his arms—even through their dueling layers of outerwear. The scent of vanilla emanating from her skin mixed with the night air and gave him a heady sort of high. He spun her around before placing her softly on the snowy ground.

They ignored Vince, who was pretending to retch, as he cut behind them to greet more friends.

Kristy spread her arms wide and tipped her head up, sticking out her tongue to catch a snowflake. "Isn't it beautiful out here?"

Ashton kept his eyes on her. "The most beautiful."

She dipped her chin and when she caught his meaning, her eyes widened, twinkling above picture-perfect rosy cheeks. She shook her head, chuckling. "You ready?"

"Born ready." Ashton held out a sled for her. "Wanna race?"

Kristy took it. "You're on."

They lined up their sleds at the top of the hill and on the count of three, they each pushed off, sending themselves careening downward. They were neck-and-neck as they skidded toward the tree line.

Kristy squealed and screamed the whole way, and Ashton laughed like he hadn't laughed in years. He felt completely free and completely alive.

At the bottom of the hill Kristy ended up barrel rolling off of her sled.

When he jogged over to make sure she was alright, she grinned up at him, her brown hair flowing out on top of the fresh, white snow like trails of chocolate syrup through vanilla ice cream.

Ashton had a thing for ice cream. And it was official. He definitely had a thing for Kristy.

Her eyes sparkled. "I think it's a tie."

He reached out his hand to help her to her feet, but instead, she yanked him down.

He landed nose-to-nose with her, bracing himself with his arms and hovering in her personal space as she giggled.

He pitched his voice, pretending to be stern. "You planned that, didn't you?"

She shrugged an innocent shrug and batted her snow-dewed eyelashes. "I guess I don't know my own strength."

"No. I guess you don't." She had no idea what she did to him. What power she held. He couldn't stop his stare from dropping to her lips. They were hanging slightly open, small puffs of air escaping from between them. He flicked his gaze back up to meet hers, using his gloved finger to clear a strand of hair away from her hooded eyes.

He wanted to kiss her.

He was aching to kiss her.

"What are you going to do about it?" She whispered the words, and as if startled by her own boldness, she bit her lip.

"Let me show you." He leaned in, bumping his nose against hers, and rubbing it back and forth. The skin-to-skin touch was like the strike of a match, and Ashton was sure the heat between them would melt every last flake of snow covering Sunrise Park.

Kristy's eyes fell closed, and she sucked in a trembling breath.

It shattered his heart in the best possible way, at once breaking him and making him whole. He bent and closed the distance between them, needing to kiss her like he needed air.

Her lips were cold when he covered them with his.

The second their mouths connected, Kristy reached around his neck and tugged him closer to her, drawing him into a deep, fiery kiss.

Kissing Kristy was an adrenaline rush like Ashton had never felt before. She was not a passive participant. She kissed him hard and sure, like she couldn't get enough of him.

Like she'd wanted to kiss him for a long time.

The awareness that she wanted this, that she wanted *him*, was intoxicating.

Because he wanted this, too.

The cold, winter's night air transformed into a sizzling, gold-threaded cocoon around them. It was as if they were the only two people in the world. He pressed himself as close to her as he could, easing himself down and to the side and shifting so he could cradle her in his arms.

Ashton had no concept of how long they stayed there, clinging to each other, savoring the exquisite first-kiss feeling.

Knowing Kristy like this, being near to her in this way, was completely new, but Ashton was fully aware that this, *this* could be it. This could be what he looked forward to. Every day for the rest of his life.

It had taken one kiss for him to know he wanted to hold her like this forever.

A throat clearing registered somewhere in the fringes of Ashton's mind. When he heard it for a second time, he pulled away from Kristy a sliver of an inch.

She moaned. "Come back."

He chuckled and brushed his lips delicately across hers once more.

She opened her eyes and blinked, dazzling him with a soft smile.

Ashton stared into the gorgeous depths of her eyes as Vince scoffed nearby.

"What did I say about PDA?"

Chapter 6

Kristy

Ashton kissed me. Ashton *kissed me*. *Ashton kissed me.*

Kristy swore she was floating as she walked into On Deck Café, the new coffee shop in town, recently opened by one of Mapleton's own, Julia Derks.

Never in Kristy's life had she felt so desired or so cherished.

Sure, having an audience of her brother hadn't been ideal, but Kristy could barely bring herself to care. All she could think about was how she wanted to kiss Ashton again. And again. And again.

Ashton stepped up behind her as the bell over the café's door jingled. "This place is great."

It was. The renovated café was warm and inviting. Mismatched chairs, tables, and booths somehow all worked together to give the place a comfortable, lived-in ambiance. A blazing fire crackled in the red-brick fireplace along the outside wall. Julia had twinkle lights dangling from the mantel and over all the windows in the small dining room space.

It was magical.

They claimed the leather loveseat that sat across from the fireplace. Kristy shed her winter coat, hat, and mittens and laid them over the arm of the seat as Ashton went up to the counter to order. He returned with two giant cups of cocoa.

He passed them both to her before slipping out of his parka and sitting down next to her. His sizable frame took up over half of the small couch, but Kristy wasn't complaining about their close proximity.

When she handed over his mug, their fingers brushed, and a shock pinged up her arm and traveled straight to her chest, sending her pulse racing.

They sat silently for a minute, each sipping their drinks. Out of the corner of Kristy's eye, she watched him cradle the cup in his large palms, slowly raising it to his mouth and taking a drawn out sip.

And she was officially jealous of a hot cocoa mug.

She wanted his hands—and lips—on her.

She glanced up into his face to find him staring back at her with an amused expression coloring his features. Her skin prickled with heat under his watch. Did he know what she was thinking about? She licked her lips and his eyes darkened, going from their trademark nautical blue to a near-black navy.

He definitely knew.

Kristy broke eye contact before she did something crazy like climb into his lap.

Because yes, she was desperate to be held by him again, but she wanted more than that, too. She wanted to get inside his head and figure out his dreams; to learn where he'd been and where he wanted to go. What made him laugh? What made his skin crawl? Kristy wanted to know everything.

She cleared her throat. "Alright. I want to hear all about what you've been up to for the last"—she checked a pretend watch on her wrist—"ten years or so since you graduated high school and left town."

"That might take a while."

"I've got all night."

Ashton tipped his chin down and side-eyed her. "Do you now?"

Kristy felt the heat of a blush wash over her face. "Keep your mind out of the gutter." She stuck her nose in the air, grinning. "Let's play twenty questions."

Ashton turned to her, his shoulder pressing into hers. "I'll play if you do. Because I want to get to know you, too."

Kristy inhaled. The thrill of talking to Ashton—of having all of his focus on her—was making her head swirl in the best possible way, all smooth and sweet like frosting on the top of a cupcake. It was exhilarating, being on the cusp of connection with a guy she respected and admired.

She nodded in agreement. "Sure. Though I'll warn you, I'm not very interesting."

Ashton frowned. "I don't believe that for a second. You're extremely interesting. To me at least."

Kristy sat back, slightly stunned. This *in-touch-with-his-feelings-and-not-afraid-to-vocalize-them* Ashton was a complete surprise.

The reserved guy she knew as her brother's best friend in high school had somehow grown into a gentleman with enough confidence and self-awareness to not only own his emotions but to express them. Yes, he was still a man of few words. But the words he did say, he made count.

Being on the receiving end of his thoughts and praise was quickly becoming Kristy's favorite hobby.

Right up there with kissing his face off.

Ashton set his drink down on the coffee table and extended his bulging arm across the back of the loveseat. "You can ask first."

Kristy leaned her head back, resting it against his toned forearm. "Okay." She wiggled her eyebrows. "Tell me about your tattoo."

Ashton snorted. "That is *not* what I was expecting you to say." He narrowed his eyes. "How do you know about my tattoo?"

Kristy held up her finger, tsking him. "Careful. Are you sure you want to use up one of your questions like that?"

He shook his head and rolled his delectable eyes. "Fine. But don't think I'm forgetting this. Be prepared for me to revisit the topic later."

Kristy brought her drink to her lips, snickering as she spoke into her cocoa mug. "Fair."

Ashton rubbed his upper arm. "My tattoo is a list of coordinates of all the places I've served." He paused, turning his head toward the fire. He looked contemplative in the flickering light.

Kristy sensed he had more to say, so she waited.

"It keeps me grounded. The places remind me of the people I've met and worked with along the way. The people are what it's all about, so I like having them close to me."

Kristy sat upright next to him, and her movement drew his gaze.

She shook her head slightly. "That's incredible, Ashton. And so meaningful. Will you add your deployment coordinates after you get home?"

Ashton dipped his chin, ignoring her praise. His cheeks colored, though, and Kristy practically swooned. Humble and hot was a lethal combination, and Ashton had it perfected.

He reached up to tuck a strand of her hair behind her ear. "You realize you just asked a second question, right?"

Kristy blinked. She was much more caught up in learning about him and enjoying every spark his finger was igniting against her cheek than she was in the rules of the game. She swallowed, trying to find her voice. "Consider it one, multi-part question." She offered him an innocent smile.

Ashton laughed, a deep, content laugh, and her heart ballooned. "You're adorable, you know that? And yes, to answer question 1b"—he shot her a pointed look—"I do plan to add coordinates when I get home. Eventually, if I settle in one place and start a family, I'll add that location, too. I figure I'll do my most important service there."

Game. Over.

Kristy had to stop from fanning herself.

Her respect for Ashton had doubled, and now his tattoo was even more of a turn on. She found herself once again at risk of jumping him, so she asked another question.

"What will you do when you're gone?"

"Nothing too exciting. We'll spend a lot of time on the ship. I'm told the hours drag. I'll probably workout twice a day just to give myself something to do."

Kristy pulled her top lip into her mouth with her teeth, trying to ward off a grin. Because, come on.

Ashton wasn't fooled. "Something tells me you like the sound of that."

Kristy ran a hand through her hair before letting it drop to his muscled arm. She squeezed his bicep. "I mean, you're not bad to look at. I can't be the first person who has told you that."

Ashton put his free hand to his chest in mock disbelief. "Kristy Vos, you *have* been checking me out."

She shoved him playfully.

He reached up and captured her hand with his, bringing it to his lips and pressing a warm kiss to her knuckles.

Dazed by the sweetness of the gesture, Kristy tried to recover her bearings. A tingle vibrated from her scalp to the soles of her shoes. She pressed the back of her hand against her cheek, at once giddy and terrified as it dawned on her that she was falling for this man. Everything about him, from his servant's heart to his muscles.

And there was nothing she could do about it.

She'd lost complete control of the situation.

ASHTON

Ashton was staring at Kristy again. He couldn't help it. He just wanted to look at her. To memorize every feature of her face. The faint lines that stretched out from the edges of her eyes when she laughed. The small beauty mark she had right on the upper corner of her lip. The exact angle of her cheek bones.

"Where were we?" Kristy stared back at him, a rose-gold blush coloring her cheeks.

Ashton brought his focus back to the conversation they were having. Talking to Kristy was easy. She made him comfortable, content to be himself. He shot her a smile. "You just finished asking, like, three questions in a row. It's my turn now."

"Go for it. You can ask me anything. I'm a pretty open book."

Ashton rubbed at his jaw. What he really wanted to know was why a woman like her was still single. Because that just didn't add up.

What had Vince told him yesterday when they were working out? Something about how she'd been hurt before? He wanted to know what happened, but he didn't want to sour their time together by bringing up a bad memory for her. So he held back. Maybe he was being spineless, but he just wanted to savor Kristy for tonight.

He snapped his fingers. "I've got it. What's your favorite ice cream flavor?"

Kristy burst out laughing. "Seriously?"

Ashton arranged his expression to look somber. "I take ice cream *very* seriously."

Kristy giggled—the sweetest sound. "Okay then. Chocolate chip cookie dough, for sure. What about you?"

"Mint chip." Ashton responded without hesitation. "You can't beat that combo of minty chocolatey goodness."

"Good pick. Next question?" Kristy sipped her cocoa, and they got lost in conversation about everything from their favorite books (she loved *Little Women*; he loved *Frankenstein*), to their most memorable college moments (she drove a car across a walking bridge and had to sweet talk the on-duty campus police officers when she got stuck; he won a kissing contest).

When he disclosed that fun fact, Kristy stopped with her mug half way to her mouth. "Is that right?"

Ashton let his head fall into his hands. It was mildly embarrassing to admit it, but yeah. He shot her a sheepish look. "Guilty. I was forced to enter the contest on a dare from some of the other ROTC guys."

Kristy set her mug down and pulled him in for a quick and fast kiss right then and there. When she released her grip on the front of his shirt, she smirked. "Just had to make sure you still had it."

Ashton lifted a corner of his mouth, trying to catch his breath. "What's the verdict?"

She raised her eyebrows. "Acceptable...but even winners need practice." She held his gaze, not shying away from taunting him. He loved it. This woman was straight up delectable. Funny. Witty. Brave. Bold. And he couldn't get enough of her.

They covered several other topics before Kristy asked a quiet question that made Ashton grimace.

"Do you want to talk about your family?"

The honest answer was nope. Not at all.

He could hardly run from the truth with Kristy, though. She was from Mapleton. She knew what happened.

He sighed. "Not really."

She stared at him with wide, understanding eyes. "We don't have to go there. I just figured it must've been hard." She placed a gentle hand on his knee. "If you ever want to talk about it, I'm here."

He covered her hand with his, squeezing. "Thank you. There's just not really much to say. It's embarrassing, you know? Everyone in Mapleton knew how unhappy my mom and dad were with each other. They didn't even try to hide it. What I never understood was why they were intent on waiting until I went to college before they finally divorced. Didn't they realize that everyone would have been better off if they'd just ended things sooner? What was the point of drawing it out? It only made all of us that much more of a spectacle."

A crease split open across Kristy's forehead as she frowned. "No one thought you were a spectacle."

"Our family was at the center of the town's gossip my entire senior year of high school." The old anger and discomfort seeped into Ashton's tone. He huffed out a calming breath. "Sorry, I don't mean to snap."

"You're allowed." Kristy smiled before turning serious again. "I just want you to know that people around here think pretty highly of you. Even though your mom and dad moved away, you'll always have a place here."

Ashton gazed at her. Would he always have a place with her? He hoped so.

"Thanks for saying that. The whole thing just makes me uncomfortable."

"I can only imagine. Where did your parents settle, anyway?"

"My dad remarried before I even finished my first year of college. He was cheating on my mom. Which made everything worse." Ashton hadn't admitted that out loud to anyone from Mapleton before now. He was sure people assumed, but he was still ashamed of his dad's behavior. "He and his new wife settled in Chicago. And my mom is doing her own thing out in Denver. Between my schedule and everyone being so spread out, I rarely see either of them."

"Well, you're always welcome here. Whenever you have time off, you can come back to Mapleton. I hope you will. My mom will ply you with lasagna." Kristy smiled, but her eyes had filled with tears.

Startled, Ashton placed his hand on her shoulder. "Kristy, what's wrong?"

He wasn't sure where her sudden burst of emotion had come from. A part of him worried that he'd scared her with the dysfunction of his family. Maybe she figured he'd end up the same as his dad. Or that he didn't know what it meant to commit because he'd had a rotten example.

She shook her head, looking into the fire. "Sorry. It's just when I think about you coming *back* here when you've got time off, I'm reminded that you're leaving. In not very long. And I don't like the thought of that." She shot him a watery grin. "I really like having you around."

Ashton's heart clenched. He really liked being around, too.

Not the best realization for someone who was signed up to leave the country in two weeks.

He softened his voice, reaching up and gently turning her chin back to face him. "I won't stay away so long this time. I promise." He used the pad of his thumb to brush away a single tear that trickled from her eye.

"Sorry. I'm being silly." She shook off his hand, and used her own fingers to dab at her lower lashes. "Let's get back to talking about happy things."

Ashton let it go, and they talked for another hour, getting to know each other.

But a niggle of doubt had weaseled its way into the back of his head. He didn't want to hurt her, and he was already making her cry.

How was this going to end well for them?

Chapter 7

"MOM?" KRISTY PULLED THE storm door firmly shut behind her as a blast of frigid air tried to follow her inside her childhood home.

"I'm in the kitchen."

Kristy followed the sound of Paige's voice to the back of the house.

"What a nice surprise, dear! I was just about to put on some tea. Would you like some?"

Kristy nodded, scooching onto one of the barstools surrounding her mom's kitchen island.

They exchanged small talk until the teapot whistled, but when they were settled, her mom ceased with the casual niceties. "What's wrong?"

"Why would anything be wrong?" Kristy tested her tea. It was still steaming, so she set it back down.

Paige arched her brow. "You rarely show up here. Uninvited. On a week night after work, no less. Not that I'm complaining, but come on. Out with it."

Kristy stared into her cup, letting the steam warm her face and trying to piece together what she was going to say. The problem was she could hardly figure out how she was feeling, much less put words to her emotions.

"You really like him, don't you, Kristy?"

Her hand jerked, and she swilled tea over the lip of her cup as she looked up.

Her mom smiled back at her, eyes full of warm, motherly affection.

Not for the first time did Kristy wonder if there was some sort of maternal instinct that allowed moms to see into their kids' souls.

"How could you tell?" Kristy finally asked.

At that, Paige let out a soft chuckle. "Oh Kristy. Don't look so troubled! It's a beautiful thing to be falling in love."

Kristy leaned an elbow on the counter and rested her face in the crook between her thumb and fingers. "How can I possibly be falling in love with him? I haven't seen him in years. We've spent less than three days together. And I don't know what I'm doing." She let her arms fall to her sides, slouching forward. "I don't want to rush into anything, but I already have, and I don't want to turn back now, but what if it's too good to be true? It's just all happening so fast, and he's leaving, Mom. Like, *leaving* leaving."

Paige placed a hand on her arm, giving her a grounding squeeze. "It's a lot, Kristy. But in my opinion, everything you just said is all quite normal, especially under the circumstances. Do you want my advice?"

Kristy nodded. She needed all the help she could get. She was way out of her element here.

"Then I'd say, let yourself feel."

"Feel?" Kristy sat upright and squinted her eyes. "What do you mean?"

"How do you feel when you're with Ashton?"

Kristy ran her teeth over her bottom lip. "Safe. Loved. Like if all I had for the rest of my life was him looking back at me, it would be enough."

"There it is." Her mom beamed. "What we feel and how our hearts react to these very moments in our lives make up the memories and the stories we get to tell the next generation. They are what make life worthwhile."

Kristy let out an unconvinced breath. "That's a beautiful sentiment, Mom. But this is reality, and he lives six states away and is leaving the country before the month is through. And I don't know the first thing about handling a long distance relationship. Or military life, for that matter."

"No, but if anyone can figure it out, it's you."

Kristy managed an appreciative smile before shaking her head. "It's the unknowns that scare me."

Her mom nodded, meaningfully. "You like to be in control, but you're also a fighter. You go after what you want. And isn't it better to go for it than to sit back and let the chance pass you by? I can tell you don't want to miss your chance with him."

Kristy pressed her eyes closed. Her mom was right, but she was terrified.

"Look, dear. Half the battle is in the choice, the decision to go down a certain path. Love is a choice, after all, and if you set your heart and mind to that man and commit to loving him well, all while he does the same for you, then you can't go wrong. Your life together will certainly be filled with ups and downs—things you can and can't control—but facing them together will make everything worthwhile."

Kristy found herself nodding. "I guess I'm extra anxious because of what happened with Declan, Mom. What if I'm wrong about Ashton and his intentions, too? What if he doesn't choose me?"

"Is Ashton worth it to you to take the chance? If so, then it's like anything, Kristy. You do it because there's nothing else to do. If you love Ashton, or think you might be falling in love with him, then you give it a shot. Let the consequences be what they may. You can't control the future, dear. We know that more than anyone."

Kristy's eyes welled with tears as her mom's gaze flicked to the family photo where her dad stood with his arm around her.

Paige looked back to Kristy, her own eyes glistening. "But you *can* control your choices. And listen here. If you make the choice to see where this goes with Ashton, then you love every part of him, whether that's the military part of his life or whatever the future may hold. Because as hard as that may be, living without him is harder."

Kristy swiped at a tear that was trailing down her cheek. "You're right...I know you're right. And I do. Love him, I mean."

"I know, dear." Her mom smiled broadly. "I knew that plain as day when I saw you two together at dinner here. And you know what the greatest part about it is?" She leaned forward.

Kristy had no idea what she was going to say. "What?"

"He loves you, too!" Her mom said it with a smile as she patted Kristy's hand and then sat back on her stool, looking pretty pleased with the whole matter.

Kristy, for her part, sat frozen in place before turning her head slowly toward her mom. "You really think so? How do you know for sure?"

"Think about it, Kristy. I think you know it, too."

Kristy thought about how Ashton treated her. How he looked her in the eyes. How he truly listened to her. How he let her see his soft side and laughed with her. How he accepted her quirks and complimented her. He was chivalrous and funny and he kissed her as if his life depended on it.

Kristy punched out a breath. "You're right."

Paige stood to grab them some cookies. "Don't sound so surprised, Kristy. He'd be a fool not to love a kind-hearted girl like yourself. Vince will be so pleased," she added with a grin.

ASHTON

Ashton leaned back against Vince's couch cushions, tossing a chicken wing bone onto the plate resting on the end table.

"So, you and my sister, huh?" Vince spoke around the wing he was currently eating. He had barbeque sauce at the corners of his mouth, and it was incredibly hard to take him seriously.

That, and the fact that this wasn't the sort of conversation Ashton preferred to have with his best friend, had him deflecting. "Yep. You sure you want to talk about this?"

Vince swallowed and grabbed a napkin, cleaning his face and turning grave. "No, I don't really, but things need to be said."

"Things like what?" Ashton shifted in his seat. He really didn't want there to be a rift between himself and Vince.

"Has she told you about Declan?"

Ashton's senses were suddenly on high alert. "Who's Declan?"

Vince twisted his mouth to the side. "I'm going to take that as a no." He scowled. "Declan is the absolute worst."

Ashton's mind reeled. He sifted through the conversations he'd had with Kristy, trying to remember what she'd told him about her past relationships. "Is he the guy she was with in law school?"

"Yeah." Vince scoffed. "Well, sort of."

Ashton was confused. "What does that even mean?"

"The guy played her in the worst possible way."

Ashton gripped the arm of Vince's couch, his hands sweating as he waited to hear more. Whatever had happened, Kristy must have downplayed it for Ashton's sake because Vince was worked up.

Vince leaned forward, resting his elbows on his knees. "Declan was a smart guy, don't get me wrong. He was in medical school when they met. His second year, I think. She had just started law school, and she fell for him hard and fast. He wanted to go into pediatrics, and they bonded over their love for kids. They were friends for a while, and then it turned into more than that. Or something. I don't know. I never asked my sister for romantic details."

Ashton gritted his teeth. He couldn't say he particularly enjoyed hearing about Kristy with another man, but he knew he wanted the full story.

"Anyway, this guy, Declan, basically reeled Kristy in by saying all the right things, or at least almost all the right things. There was just one problem. He told her that since he was so swamped with med school and she was so swamped with law school, they should hold off officially dating until they'd both graduated. He said he didn't want to distract her, and he really needed to be focused, too."

Ashton blew out a breath. He waited, a wave of dread washing over him. There had to be something else. "Okay?"

Vince's scowl deepened the more he talked about Declan. "The problem was he never officially broke up with her. No, he strung her along. Kept her close enough so that when he needed her, he knew she would always be there to answer his call, to come over, to cuddle up and play house, but then the second he'd had his fill, he'd fall back on their 'agreement'"—Vince made air quotes—"as an excuse to not be there for her, or to not take any of the next steps in the relationship. She'd find out that he was out with all sorts of other female friends. Basically he wanted her, but he wanted no strings attached."

If someone had a way to see into Ashton's heart at that very moment, he was sure they'd find his blood literally boiling—full-fledged, blowing the top off the pot, splattering every-where, boiling.

Vince wasn't done. "Kristy made excuses for what he was doing. Chalking it up to stress, or saying that it was good for him to get out with friends. She believed him when he said that if they just got through school they could move forward as a normal couple. He told her she was the kind of girl people like him married. Wink, wink, nudge, nudge." Vince shook his head sadly. "She stayed true to him, closed herself off from dating anyone else during school, and waited for the day they could be together. She had their whole lives planned out, and you can probably guess how it ended."

Ashton was so mad, he couldn't respond with words. He gave Vince a single nod.

"Law school graduation came, and he didn't even show up for her ceremony. She went to his apartment and found him in bed with another med-school student. He then had the gall to tell her that he'd be fine if the roles were reversed and he'd found her with another man. She ended things then and there, but she gave up three years of her life to him, and she was left with nothing but a hurt heart and a pile of wrecked plans."

Vince lapsed into stony silence as the story settled over them like a pall.

Ashton could not fathom how someone could be so disrespect-ful to a woman. To any woman, but especially to someone like Kristy, who was so full of life and love to give.

He raked a hand through his hair. "Vince, you have to know I would *never* treat Kristy like that."

Vince looked up at him, more serious than he'd ever seen him. "Of course I know that, but I don't want my sister to get hurt again...in *any* way. Don't you see?"

Ashton stared back at him, uneasiness beating around in his gut.

"I see how you are with her. How she is with you. She never looked at Declan the way she looks at you. But is that enough? With your job and your lifestyle? Is she just going to be waiting around for you, too? And what if something happens, Ash?" Vince held out his hands in question, letting them drop to the arms of his chair with a hollow thump and leaving unspoken the risks associated with Ashton's job in the military.

Ashton ground his teeth together, hating the valid points Vince was making. "What am I supposed to do?"

Vince shrugged. "I don't know. But ever since our dad died, I've taken it upon myself to watch out for Kristy. I'm asking for your help with that. You're a good man, so just think this through before you make my sister fall completely in love with you. While it may be all fun and exciting now, if she's going to end up heartbroken in the end, it's not worth it."

Ashton nodded stiffly. His phone buzzed in his pocket, and Vince rose to leave the room.

"Think about what I said, okay? I only want what's best for both you and Kristy."

"I know. Thanks, man." Ashton pulled up the message on his phone, and his heart dropped to the floor. It was almost as if this was his answer.

Vince paused in the doorway to the kitchen and glanced back at him. "What is it?"

"We're deploying early. I need to catch a flight back to North Carolina tonight."

Chapter 8

KRISTY

AFTER WORK ON WEDNESDAY evening, Kristy drove directly to her brother's house. She picked her way up Vince's icy front walkway, careful to avoid a fall. She had her running shoes dangling from her gloved fingers. She'd never gotten Ashton's phone number, and she really didn't want to make plans through her brother, so she decided to show up in person.

She knocked briskly, puffing out white clouds of air and shifting her weight between her legs to stay warm as she waited to be let in.

Vince opened the door, looking more pensive than usual. "Hey, Kristy. Come on in." He pulled the door open fully and let her walk inside. "You're going for a run through Mapleton at this hour? It's pretty slick out there, isn't it?"

She peeked around, looking for Ashton, but he was nowhere in sight. "Yeah, I was hoping to convince Ashton to come with me. Is he here?"

Vince wouldn't meet her eye. "Uh, no. Actually, he's not."

"Oh. Is he out seeing friends or something?"

"No. He left."

"Left?" Kristy frowned. "What are you talking about? He's here through the weekend."

Vince scratched his cheek, still avoiding her gaze. "He was supposed to be, but he got word last night that they're deploying earlier than expected. He had to get back to base."

The air in the living room turned to sludge, and Kristy had a hard time breathing it in. Her ears started buzzing as she slumped down into one of Vince's side chairs, her limbs feeling heavy. "So he's gone, just like that? I don't understand. Why didn't he call me?"

Vince started walking toward the kitchen but changed direction and walked around the backside of the couch. He glanced beyond her to the door, as if looking for someone to rescue him. "I don't know, but he asked me to give you this." Vince bent and picked up a white envelope from the end table, crossing the room again and handing it over to her.

Kristy took it with trembling hands.

"I'll–uh, be in my room if you need me." Vince motioned for the stairs and then made a beeline away from her.

Kristy took a deep breath and ripped open the envelope.

Dear Kristy,

I don't know how to begin saying all the things I want to say to you. So first, I hope you know that I think you are the most incredible woman I've ever laid eyes on. You are beautiful and smart and kind, and when I'm in your presence, I feel more alive. You have a way of making people around you feel like they matter, and I admire that.

I want you to know that you matter to me. So very much. And that's why I have to end things between us before they go any further. Since you're reading this, you already know that my deployment got moved up. It kills me not to say goodbye to you in person or even over the phone, but I really think a clean break is best for me, and I hope you'll come to see it's best for you.

You have so much to give, Kristy. I couldn't live with myself if I was the one holding you back. My life is so uncertain, and you deserve someone who is there for you. I can't be there for you, and I can't ask you to wait until I'm able to be.

I never intended to lead you on. I guess my heart got out in front of my head for a bit. I don't regret one second of the time I spent with you. Thank you for sharing your heart with me, if only for a brief while.

I'll treasure these days. Keep me in your prayers.

Ashton

Kristy blinked and reread Ashton's letter, searching the lines for something, anything, that would make this make sense.

There had to be some sort of mistake. What did he mean he hadn't intended to lead her on? He hadn't! At least not until this moment, when he left without a word.

Kristy scrambled to her feet and took the steps three at a time to get to Vince's room. "Vince!" She pounded on his door. "Open up this—"

The door swung open. "Easy there. You're a person, not a jackhammer. And I happen to like this door."

Vince was trying to be funny, but Kristy ignored him. She held up the letter and waved it in front of his face. "Did you know about this?"

Vince eyed her warily, his gaze bouncing between her and the sheet of paper she clutched. "About what?"

"Everything! Ashton broke up with me in this letter"—she shook it so that it crinkled for good measure—"because he didn't want me to wait around for him. Why would he think I was waiting around for him?"

Vince held out his hands in front of his chest. "Let's sit."

He led the way back downstairs to the living room and dropped onto the couch.

Kristy didn't think she could sit still. She stood opposite of him, gripping the letter and wishing it would turn into some kind of portkey to take her straight to Ashton.

Vince rubbed his hands up and down the legs of his sweatpants.

"Well?" She started pacing. "What happened?"

Vince's face was awash with guilt. "Now, don't be mad."

Kristy rounded on him, curling her arms over her head. "Oh Vince, what did you do? Did you tell him he couldn't date me? Tell me you didn't."

"No, of course I didn't tell him he couldn't date you. I said you were both adults and could make your own decisions. I just mentioned what happened with Declan and told him I didn't want to see history repeat itself."

"You WHAT?"

"Hey!" Vince stood up and pointed at her, his brow lowering over piercing eyes, the same color as her own. "You're my baby sister, Kristy. I'm trying to look out for you. Declan"—he said the name like a curse—"treated you like dirt. You waited around for him, planned your whole future with him, and then he betrayed you. I saw how it affected you, and I told Ashton what happened so he would understand why I was asking him not to hurt you like that."

Still holding Ashton's letter, Kristy pressed the palms of her hands into her eye sockets. The skin around her eyes stung, and a painfully hot knob was wedged in the back of her throat. She sucked in a deep, rickety breath and counted to five before letting it go. She repeated the calming exercise twice more, but it didn't help her feel any better. "Oh no. Oh no. Oh no."

"Kristy. I'm sorry. I was just trying to look out for you. Ashton's lifestyle and yours don't mesh, and I didn't want to see you get your heart ripped out again. Neither did he."

Kristy dropped her hands. "Vince, you know Ashton, right? He's your oldest, best friend."

"Yeah?" Vince stretched out the word, tilting his head as if he was trying to figure out where she was going with this train of thought.

"So do you think he's a lot like Declan?"

"What?! Absolutely not. Declan is a dumbas—"

"Exactly." Kristy cut him off. "And Ashton is not. In fact, he's the exact opposite of that." She held her chin up, drawing her brother's eye and daring him to dispute her.

Vince opened his mouth and shut it again. His eyes were stuck wide open. "You're right." He blinked and bowed his head. "Oh man. I'm sorry, Kristy. I swear I didn't tell him he had to end things. I just told him to be careful. He wrote the letter and left all on his own. If he would have asked my advice, I would have told him to at least call you." Vince grimaced, looking defeated.

Kristy's stomach seized painfully, knotting with frantic desire to see Ashton, to try to work things out.

She started pacing the room again, her mind racing. Vince knew her well enough not to say a word as she worked through her options.

Eventually, she blew out a lungful of air and turned toward him, a plan forming. "It's okay, Vince. It'll be okay. It has to be. But now, I need your help."

ASHTON

Ashton stood with his hands on his hips, staring down the mound of military-issued gear piled high on his bed. Maybe if he glared at it hard enough, it would pack itself.

He sighed, running a hand through his hair as he sat down on his bed, ignoring the pile of clothes beneath him. He felt all out of sorts. It had been four days since he left Mapleton on the evening flight back to North Carolina, and he hadn't heard anything from Kristy.

Not that he expected to.

He felt like a coward for leaving her without saying goodbye or explaining himself beyond the letter, but he was trying to do what was best for both of them, and if he'd seen her, or even just heard her voice, he would have waivered in his resolve.

And he was not about to be like his father and drag things out only for everyone to get hurt in the end.

Vince had texted a few days earlier to ask when he was shipping out, and Ashton had wanted to ask after Kristy, but he refrained. He needed to move on, and he couldn't dwell on what might have been.

Still, the whiplash of having Kristy and then losing her made him dizzy with regret. He had a feeling that at night on the ship, in his rack, squished into a stateroom with three other guys, his mind would wander to the woman who held his whole heart back in Wisconsin.

Ashton checked his phone. It was eight o'clock. He had twelve hours before he had to be at Building C, ready to leave the country for the better part of the next year.

He pushed off his knees and stood up again. He dragged his sea bag out of the small closet in his room and started folding his uniform trousers, rolling them up to save space and shoving them into the bottom of his bag.

He had half his things packed thirty minutes later when a knock sounded on his door.

"Food. Finally." Ashton grabbed his wallet off the kitchen counter and strode to the front door. He'd ordered pizza as his final dinner stateside. It would be a long time before he'd get to have his favorite food...at least the way he was used to enjoying it—hot and greasy, straight out of a cardboard box.

He opened the door with one hand, flipping through his wallet with the other and trying to dig out a five dollar bill to tip his delivery guy.

"Hi."

Ashton's head flew up. He gripped the door frame, his knees locking and his heart lurching up, down, and all around in his chest. "Kristy."

She stood staring back at him, her thumbs looped through the straps of the backpack she wore. Her long, brown hair was tied up in a messy ponytail. A few stray wisps framed the milky skin of her face. He wanted to lunge for her. To pull her to him and kiss her. But he'd forfeited that right, and she looked like she had something to get off her chest.

She stared at him expectantly. "Can I come in?"

His hand slipped down the edge of the door. "Uh, yeah. Of course. Sorry. I'm just—what are you doing here? How are you here?"

She walked into his living room, and his head nearly exploded. He hadn't let himself dream she'd ever be in his space, and yet here she was. His mind took off, wondering what she thought of it, what she'd do to fix it up, to make it her own.

To make it their own.

He reigned himself in. He needed to shut those kinds of thoughts down. There was a reason he'd ended things. It was the only way he could be sure he wouldn't cause Kristy pain. He wasn't going to treat her like Declan did. Or like his dad treated his mom.

Then again, there was a big difference here, wasn't there? Because he was well on his way to loving Kristy, and that changed everything.

Ashton stilled.

That changed *everything*.

He sucked in a hard breath as Kristy rounded on him.

She fished a worn sheet of loose leaf paper out of the back pocket of her jeans. "I came to talk to you about this." She held it up, and he realized it was his letter. "You left town. Without talking to me. Without saying goodbye. And that's not okay with me."

Did she fly all the way to the east coast to chastise him? He deserved it, but he'd be lying if he said he wasn't hoping for reconciliation instead of retaliation. How had he screwed this all up so badly?

Ashton's heart sunk to the floor. "I was only doing what I thought you needed. I—"

She held up her hand to stop his sputtering. "I have a lot of stuff I want to say, so just let me get it all out, alright?"

He nodded. He owed her that.

"I know you were doing what you thought was best. I know you were trying to protect me and my heart. You wouldn't be you if you didn't. But you don't get to decide what I need without consulting me."

She pointed at his chest. "You left without giving me a say. You decided that we were better off apart, and you didn't even ask me what I thought. That's not cool with me. Because you didn't give me a chance to tell you that I want to be with you. That I'm willing to risk any and all heartache that comes with a relationship with you."

Ashton didn't dare breathe. He didn't say a word. Not yet. He kept his gaze locked on her.

Kristy took a step toward him and held her arms out to her sides, palms up. "I don't know the first thing about being in a relationship with someone in the military, and yeah, that scares the heck out of me. I might be really bad at it sometimes, and maybe you'll get annoyed by me, but I don't care. I'll figure it out. I *want* to figure it out. Because I want you, Ashton. I've always wanted you."

Kristy's chest heaved up and down. Her eyes were ablaze with the same passion she'd poured into every one of her words.

"Are you finished?"

"For now, yes."

"Good." He closed the gap between them and swept Kristy up into his arms, crashing his lips against hers.

Chapter 9

KRISTY

KRISTY SAID HER PIECE and had barely caught her breath when Ashton ripped it right back away from her. He clasped her head between his hands and claimed her lips as if they were his most prized possession.

The fire burning between them would keep her warm for days.

Weeks.

Months.

Years.

A lifetime.

She wouldn't have it any other way.

Kristy melted into his kiss, so relieved to be in his arms again before he got onto a ship and sailed away.

When they came up for air, Ashton pressed a gentle kiss against her forehead. "Thank you," he whispered, his feather-light breath tickling her skin. "I'm sorry for being so stupid."

She smiled, tucking her head against his chest. "You're not stupid. I mean, maybe you were a little bit, but I understand what you were trying to do. Just promise me that from now on, we'll make decisions about this relationship together."

"I promise." He leaned her away from him, looking her up and down as if trying to verify that she was real. "I can't believe you're here."

"I would have been here sooner, but I got lost on base. Everything around here looks exactly the same, and nothing is labeled well. It also took me a while to get past the gate guard." Kristy made an exasperated face, and Ashton chuckled. "Like I said, I might be sort of bad at this military girlfriend thing."

Maybe she was being presumptuous, calling herself his girlfriend when they hadn't had a *define the relationship* conversation. But she figured since he didn't turn her away after she took a flight across the country and bore her soul to him, she could claim the title.

Ashton kissed her nose, reassuring her further. "You're perfect just the way you are. You don't have to be anything you're not. I just want you to be you."

Kristy stood straighter and took a deep breath. "Okay." It felt good to hear him say it. "It's going to take some getting used to for me, the whole not being in control thing."

"Wait, you like to be in control?" Ashton tipped his chin down at her. "I had no idea."

"Very funny." She punched him lightly, her hand stopping against his rock solid stomach. She let her fingers trail up and down, counting the ridges of his abs beneath his shirt. "Since I'm here, do you need help getting anything ready?"

"Actually, yes." He twined his fingers with hers and pulled her across the room, grabbing a printed list off his kitchen counter. "Want to help me pack?"

"Are you kidding me?" Kristy snatched the paper away from him, scanning it quickly. "Lists are my love language. I was born for this."

Ashton grinned, and Kristy followed him into his bedroom.

It was sparsely decorated with a crucifix hanging on one wall and a digital clock on the nightstand next to his bed. The bed was covered with camouflage clothing. On the floor were two different pairs of tactical boots, a stack of books, and countless pairs of rolled socks.

Kristy clapped her hands. "Let's get to work!"

They laughed and talked as they got Ashton ready to go. Kristy forced herself to be present in the moment with him. She didn't let herself think ahead to the fact that they were getting his bags ready because he was leaving. She knew that, but she didn't want to get sad. Not yet. She wanted to savor each minute with him—to squeeze out every ounce of the joy.

They paused to share the pizza Ashton had ordered before she arrived, and when he was all packed, they cuddled up on the couch to watch a movie.

As she rested against him, wiggling herself into the cleft of his shoulder and loving how he folded her into himself with his big strong arm, Kristy took a mental picture, logging each of her senses in the moment, knowing she was going to relive this night every night for the next half a year until she could be back in Ashton's arms again.

Chapter 10

To: Kristy Vos <KRISTYVOS@MAPLETONLAW.COM>

From: Captain Klink, Ashton <ashton.klink@usmc.org>

Subject: Ahoy from the Atlantic!

January 11, 9:54 pm

Dear Kristy,

I miss you. I know it hasn't even been a week since we said goodbye, but it's true. Today has been more of the same—just getting acclimated to the ship and going to a lot of meetings that are way more relevant to the pilots than they are to us auxiliary personnel. I did finally get my sea bag unpacked and I found the stack of letters you somehow snuck into my bag.

My stomach did an actual summersault when I saw them. It was so thoughtful of you, and the promise of getting to read something new and handwritten from you each week is what's going to get me through the endless hours on this big hunk of metal. I'm already looking forward to my next letter. We'll see how long my resolve lasts...fair warning, I might crack and read them all at once, even though you dated them. You're amazing.

We've been told to expect rough seas today and for the next couple of days as we cross the Atlantic. One of my roommates, Jason, is in his rack lamenting the wasted day. I don't really mind much, it's just another day closer to seeing you again.

I'm going to lie down and try to catch some shut eye myself. I just wanted to say hi. I can't wait to hear from you.

Always,

Ashton


```
To: Captain Klink, Ashton <ashton.klink@usmc.org>
From: Kristy Vos <kristyvos@mapletonlaw.com>
Subject: re: Ahoy from the Atlantic!
January 12, 7:31 am
```


Dear Ashton,

I'm glad you liked the letters. And I'm glad you found them! I was starting to worry that maybe I'd hid them too well. ☺

Life in Mapleton is pretty much business as usual. I've been working my normal hours, and we had family dinner at my mom's house last night. No lasagna this week, but she did whip up a mean batch of chicken noodle soup with homemade bread. She spoils me, and she assured me she'll spoil you with as much food as you can handle as soon as you get back here. You'll be happy to know that Vince has been groveling. I think he still feels bad that he played a part in our, ahem, hiccup. It's good for him to be knocked down a peg or two, don't you think?

I miss you, too. A lot. Anytime something noteworthy happens, you're the first person I want to share it with. I think about what you might be doing all the time. I've been reading up on all things military and Marine Corps. I'm so proud of you.

I'm going to send you the pictures we took at your place via snail mail. I want you to have something to remind you of me in your rack. Hopefully I can figure out how to correctly put the FPO address of the ship on my package. Watch for a box from Mapleton in the next few weeks.

I've got to run now...literally. The snow let up and I'm going to try to get out for a quick three miles. In case you're wondering, I spend most of my workouts daydreaming of you and looking forward to the day I can stalk you and your muscles in the gym again...

Muscle deprived in Mapleton,

Kristy

```
To: Kristy Vos <kristyvos@mapletonlaw.com>
From: Captain Klink, Ashton <ashton.klink@usmc.
org>
Subject: More muscles for you
January 12, 7:03 pm
```

I will never turn down mail. Anything to be closer to you. I wish I could kiss you right now. You're so beautiful. But let me make one thing clear...I don't need a picture to remember you by. Anytime I have a spare minute, I conjure up the mental image of your smile and imagine myself gazing into your eyes, and my day is instantly improved.

In case *you* were wondering, I've been spending two hours in the gym each day. It's something productive to do to pass the time, and it breaks up the planning meetings, which are what seem to fill the rest of our days. Lots of planning for potential practice missions. We'll see if any of it comes to fruition. I hope it does. I'm already itching to get off the ship. If I do, I might be able to video chat with you.

Maybe I'll even flex for you on camera?

Always,

Ashton

```
To: Captain Klink, Ashton <ashton.klink@usmc.org>
From: Kristy Vos <kristyvos@mapletonlaw.com>
Subject: re: More muscles for you
January 13, 8:14 pm
```

Umm, okay. Not only are you ripped, but you also managed to send flowers to my apartment on the longest day ever?! On that note, sorry I didn't email you this morning. I was in the office early, and the day got away from me. Ugh. But back to the flowers. How did you pull that off?! I was just settling in for a nice evening of binge watching old episodes of Friends (the blooper reels are the best, if you haven't seen them), and I got a knock on my door. I armed myself with a rolling pin (safety first), but alas, it was just the flower delivery guy from Roses and More.

I'm attaching a picture of the arrangement. It's gorgeous. Seriously, you did not have to do that. But I'll have you know I already tucked the note from you under my pillow, and I've been carrying the flowers with me from room to room (like Meg Ryan does in *You've Got Mail*, you know?) because they make me feel close to you.

I want to be close to you. And your muscles. But mostly just you. All of you. Okay, I'm stopping now.

Seriously, thank you. Thank you for thinking of me and for making me smile, even though we're an ocean apart.

Kristy

```
To: Captain Klink, Ashton <ashton.klink@usmc.org>
From: Kristy Vos <kristyvos@mapletonlaw.com>
Subject: One more thing
January 13, 8:17 pm
```

I know it's a long way off, but is it okay with you if I fly to North Carolina for your homecoming?

Say the word, and I'll be there.

Kristy

To: Kristy Vos <kristyvos@mapletonlaw.com>
From: Captain Klink, Ashton <ashton.klink@usmc.org>
Subject: re: One more thing
January 14, 3:02 am

Yes, please. Already counting down the days.
Ashton

·❤·❤·❤·❤·❤·

To: Kristy Vos <kristyvos@mapletonlaw.com>
From: Captain Klink, Ashton <ashton.klink@usmc.org>
Subject: I love you
April 23, 4:19 pm

Hi sweetheart,

Is it okay with you if I call you sweetheart? I hope so. We're back on the ship after a week in Djibouti. It was a good training mission. Nice for our team to work together to set up the mobile airstrips, and good for the pilots to get some practice in, too. It was mostly so great to be able to call you over the satellite phone. Hearing your voice is something I'll never take for granted. Thanks for answering...even though it was the middle of the night for you.

As for me, lying out in the desert under the stars, I had a lot of time to think about us and the future. I want to get back home so badly. I feel this sort of pulling in my chest. Like there's a physical hand yanking me back in your direction. It's a good sign, I think. It means I've got something to look forward to. For so long, my life has been about this job. And it's a good job, and I'm glad to do it. But lately, I've been wondering what's next, you know? What will life look like in a year or two? How do I want it to look?

How do *you* want it to look?

All I kept coming back to out there in the middle of nowhere was the fact that I want you by my side.

I'm in love with you, Kristy. I should have said it over the phone, but I was just so damn overwhelmed to be talking to you, my words got all caught up in my throat. But I love you. I think I've loved you for a long time. I wish I could see your face when you read these words. I wish I could follow them up with a kiss, but I can't keep them to myself anymore, so I hope it's okay that I said them anyway.

Thanks for putting up with me.

All my love,

Ashton

To: Captain Klink, Ashton <ashton.klink@usmc.or g>

From: Kristy Vos <kristyvos@mapletonlaw.com>

Subject: re: I love you

April 23, 10:08 pm

I love you, too, Ashton. I've fallen madly in the love with the man you are.

As for the future, I really don't care what it brings as long as we're in it together. It's pretty crazy, but since dating you, I can feel my controlling tendencies slipping away. It's like it took something as major as a deployment, where the guy I'm in love with is on the other side of the world and I have zero control over the situation, to make me see that there are more important things in life than worrying about everything unfolding perfectly.

Perfect is such a relative word, anyway, isn't it? My life will be perfect for me as long as you're in it.

I love you,

Kristy

P.S. Thanks for saying it first. I've wanted to sign off my emails with my love pretty much since the day you left, and I know it's the twenty-first century and I'm all for female empowerment, but yeah, I wanted to hear it from you first. ;)

P.P.S. YES you can call me sweetheart. You can call me whatever you want. I like that I'm the one on the receiving end of your pet names. Makes me feel all sorts of special. I love you again.

```
To: Kristy Vos <kristyvos@mapletonlaw.com>
From: Captain Klink, Ashton <ashton.klink@usmc.org>
Subject: Long day…made better because of YOU
April 25, 12:10 am
```

Kristy,

All day I've felt like I could fly higher than the jets that take off from this ship. You love me…and that's unbelievable and exhilarating. Thank you. Is it weird to say thank you for your love? I'm so grateful. I'll do everything I can to be worthy of it...every day, for as long as you'll let me.

I'm writing pretty late tonight, or I guess, this morning. It's been busy here. The ship was having an issue, and my team had a rather creative idea that might fix it. After a day's work and talking to a lot of different parties we developed a partial solution. Unfortunately it won't completely alleviate the issue at hand, but it helped, and a lot of folks appreciated our efforts. It's sure nice to sit down now, though.

We're already four months into this thing, do you realize that? I can't help but think of that Bon Jovi song because we're halfway there. Thanks for sticking with me, and for being such a rock. Watch for your weekly flower delivery tomorrow. ☺

I'm going to cut this email short so I can catch some shut eye, but know I'll go to bed dreaming of you.

I love you (it's never going to get old saying that),
Ashton

P.S. How are you feeling about your race? One more week of training, right? I wish I could be there to cheer you on!


```
To: Captain Klink, Ashton <ashton.klink@usmc.or
g>
From: Kristy Vos <kristyvos@mapletonlaw.com>
Subject: re: Long day...made better because of YOU
April 25, 1:31 pm
```


A couple things. First, thanks for getting that song stuck in my head for the duration of the day. What an earworm. Second, I'm not at all surprised that you and your team are doing good work out there. Have I mentioned how proud I am of you? Third, me and Jake, the flower delivery guy, are on a first name basis. He and his wife, Charlotte, who own the shop, want to meet you when you get home. You are the sweetest man, you know that? It's not just me who thinks so, either. Jake and Charlotte agree, in case you were wondering. ;)

I'm feeling good about my race. It'll be good to just get out there, you know? But I feel ready, so I guess that's all I can hope for.

I'm off to add *Livin' on a Prayer* to my running playlist now.

I love you,

Kristy

To: Captain Klink, Ashton <ashton.klink@usmc.org>
From: Kristy Vos <kristyvos@mapletonlaw.com>
Subject: No subject
April 25, 11:56 pm

Hey you,

I can't sleep. I made the mistake of watching the news tonight, and they reported on how ISIS is targeting and trying to pick off military members and their families. Rationally, I know you're pretty safe over there, but I just really miss you, and I want you here.

Sorry for being a baby and for flooding your inbox today.

I love you,

Kristy

To: Kristy Vos <kristyvos@mapletonlaw.com>

```
From: Captain Klink, Ashton <ashton.klink@usmc.
org>
Subject: re: No subject
April 26, 9:04 am
```

Kristy, you're not a baby. You never have to apologize to me for how you're feeling. Honestly, you've handled this separation like a champ, and everything you're feeling is normal. I wish I could kiss you and tell you it was all okay in person, but for now, you're going to have to put up with another email.

I don't want to belittle your concerns. Your feelings are valid, but I will encourage you not to give too much thought to what you hear on the news. We won't have anything to do with what's going on in France, and no one is coming after a Captain or his hot girlfriend...let's rejoice in the fact that I'm not very important. ☺

That being said, ISIS really is a fascinating and capable enemy. I've had a lot of access to more sensitive intelligence briefings on the ship. They are definitely impressive and appropriately respected by the Marine Corps. I trust our military and our leadership, though. You can trust me, too. I know it's easier said than done, but try not to worry too much about our involvement.

I hope you were able to get some sleep. I wish I could kiss your morning face right now. You're so beautiful. I can't wait to hear from you again—you can always email me. I miss you all the time.

I love you,

Ashton

```
To: Captain Klink, Ashton <ashton.klink@usmc.or
g>
From: Kristy Vos <kristyvos@mapletonlaw.com>
```

```
Subject: re: re: No subject
April 26, 10:01 pm
```

Thank you for your message, Ashton. And can I just say I'm so grateful the internet connection on the ship was strong enough to get to chat with you in real time earlier today, too. It was just what my heart needed.

You're the best. Thanks for talking me down from the ledge. I like to think that we balance each other out pretty well. What do you think?

I'm going to sleep now. I'll be thinking of you, like always.

I love you,

Kristy

·♥·♥·♥·♥·♥·

```
To: Captain Klink, Ashton <ashton.klink@usmc.org>
  From: Kristy Vos <kristyvos@mapletonlaw.com>
  Subject: It's gonna be MAY
  April 30, 7:45 pm
```

Did you catch that Justin Timberlake reference in my subject line? He's so dreamy, isn't he?

Race day is tomorrow, but I just wanted to send a quick note to celebrate the fact that we made it to the end of another month. Which means I'm one month closer to being in your arms.

I can't wait.

I love you more than I love *NSYNC,

Kristy

```
To: Kristy Vos <kristyvos@mapletonlaw.com>
```

```
From: Captain Klink, Ashton <ashton.klink@usmc.
org>
Subject: re: It's gonna be MAY
May 1, 5:14 am
```

Good luck today, Kristy! You'll be great. Also, thanks for saying you love me more than *NSYNC. For a second, I was afraid I was going to have to come home and fight a boyband for your affection.

Maybe this is a good time to tell you I can now bench 225lbs pretty easily. That's two 45lb plates on either side of the bar. Am I impressing you enough to take your mind off JT? I hope so. ☺

I can't wait to hear how your race goes. I'll be cheering you on from the Mediterranean.

I love you more than '90s Justin Timberlake loved bleach-tipped curls,

Ashton

```
To: Captain Klink, Ashton <ashton.klink@usmc.or
g>
From: Kristy Vos <kristyvos@mapletonlaw.com>
Subject: re: re: It's gonna be MAY
May 1, 4:37 pm
```

Hey handsome,

I did it! The race went great! Thanks for thinking of me. Maybe when you get back, we can go for runs together...that is, if you aren't too weighed down by all the new muscles.

Don't mind me, I'll just be over here panting...because of the half marathon, of course...nothing to do with the image of your biceps that won't leave my mind.

Hot, bothered, and happy about it,
Kristy

·♥·♥·♥·♥·♥·

```
To: Kristy Vos <kristyvos@mapletonlaw.com>
 From: Captain Klink, Ashton <ashton.klink@usmc.
org>
 Subject: Happy Fourth of July!
 July 4, 6:15 am
```

Hi Kristy,

I'm thinking of you today. I wish I could be in Mapleton so we could go to the Fourth of July Festival together. Can you pencil me in for next year? I'd love to steal a kiss from you on the top of the Ferris wheel, hold your hand as we strolled around the park, and wrap you in my arms for a moonlit dance after the fireworks.

Can you tell I've had some time for daydreaming this week? It'll be another slow day here today. It's a no-fly day, actually. About once a week everything stops so that we can enjoy the off-time, and this week, they timed it with the holiday to try to boost morale. Most of us are pretty ready to be off this ship. They say this is the hardest month, because we're close to coming home, but not quite close enough that we can start an official countdown or anything. Especially since exact dates are all still up in the air.

You're still planning to be there when I get home, right? I'm trying not to sound desperate here, but if I'm being honest, sometimes it's the thought of seeing you again that gets me through the day.

I love you madly,

Ashton

```
To: Captain Klink, Ashton <ashton.klink@usmc.or
g>
  From: Kristy Vos <kristyvos@mapletonlaw.com>
  Subject: re: Happy Fourth of July!
  July 4, 10:59 am
```

I wish I could teleport you here so we could enjoy everything you just described *today*. That all sounds amazing. But you don't have to steal kisses from me. I'll gladly give them to you for free.

You get the prize. I'm sure you're going stir crazy, and it seems unfair that on a day we celebrate our independence—eating grilled food and sending off fireworks—you and your colleagues are stuck in foreign waters, working. I know you'd never complain, but I can tell how ready you are to be done.

Hang in there, love. I wouldn't miss your homecoming for anything. So keep on dreaming about it. I am, too. But I'm pretty sure all of my dreams are going to pale in comparison to the real feeling of seeing you again.

I can't wait 'til then.

I love you,

Kristy

·♥·♥·♥·♥·♥·

```
To: Kristy Vos <kristyvos@mapletonlaw.com>
  From: Captain Klink, Ashton <ashton.klink@usmc.
org>
  Subject: Homecoming information (!!!!!!!!)
  August 2, 2:09 pm
```

Hey sweetheart,

I passed along your contact information to our unit's FRO (that's the Family Readiness Officer). Her name is Jenn, and she's going to email you all the details you need to know about when we'll be arriving back on base.

I can hardly believe I'm typing those words. All I can think is—it's about dang time.

Jenn'll be able to answer any of your questions. Sorry I can't be the one to tell you all the things...we've just got to keep the appropriate security measures in place.

But the countdown is officially on.

You're amazing, and I love you,

Ashton


```
To: Captain Klink, Ashton <ashton.klink@usmc.or
g>
From: Kristy Vos <kristyvos@mapletonlaw.com>
Subject: re: Homecoming information (!!!!!!!!)
August 2, 11:22 pm
```

Ashton, I'm screaming. I'm so freaking excited. I already booked a plane ticket, and I'm coming for YOU.

Now to figure out what to wear. ;)

I love you,

Kristy


```
To: Kristy Vos <kristyvos@mapletonlaw.com>
From: Captain Klink, Ashton <ashton.klink@usmc.
org>
```

```
Subject:    re:    re:    Homecoming    information
(!!!!!!!!)
August 3, 6:17 am
```

You're killing me, Kristy. Now all day I'm going to be thinking about you in a dress, standing there looking like an angel, waiting to welcome me home.

I'm not going to get anything done. Oh well. These are going to be the longest days of my life.

I love you,

Ashton


```
To: Captain Klink, Ashton <ashton.klink@usmc.or
g>
From: Kristy Vos <kristyvos@mapletonlaw.com>
Subject:  re:  re:  re:  Homecoming  information
(!!!!!!!!)
August 3, 12:31 pm
```

0:)

Chapter 11

Kristy

Kristy stared out of the airplane hangar. The large, retractable doors were open, revealing a wide slab of blacktop and concrete. The August sun shone bright in the clear, Carolina blue sky, and it was pushing one hundred degrees.

The hangar was hot and loud and wonderful.

To her right, maintenance Marines were hard at work doing their daily tasks to keep the machines in prime flying condition. The constant sound of metal grinding against metal was intense, and it was hard for Kristy to believe that these guys were just going about their business as usual, completely unfazed by the dressed-up group of civilians overtaking their workspace and dripping with anticipation to welcome home their service members.

To Kristy's left, an oversized American flag hung from the far wall, filling her with patriotic pride. The families of the men and women who had been deployed with Ashton flitted back and forth in front of it, shouting to be heard over the noise.

Anticipation crackled in the air, filling the humid hangar with an addicting hum of electricity.

"Here, sis. Drink some water."

Kristy turned around to find Vince holding out a water bottle for her.

"Thanks." She grabbed it and took a swig.

"I don't understand how you're so calm. I'm going out of mind here." Vince wiped the sweat from his brow. "Why do they keep getting delayed?"

Vince had insisted upon flying out with her for Ashton's homecoming. While she didn't relish the idea of having him looking on for what she was dreaming up to be a very passionate embrace after eight long months apart, it warmed her heart that her brother wanted to help. She'd given him the official role of homecoming photographer. She had a feeling she was going to want to remember this day for a very long time.

Kristy shrugged, and sat down next to Vince. "Who knows? Things happen on the ship. And they had to load up all their stuff onto the ospreys that'll fly them ashore. They're getting dropped off across base, and then they'll be bussed here to us. It's not surprising that they ran into a snag. Don't worry. They'll get here."

Vince scoffed. "Listen to you, all relaxed and going with the flow."

Kristy laughed. "I'm going to see Ashton today. I'd wait another eight months, if that's what it took, but he's coming home today. He's so close now. I'm not going to get bent out of shape over a minor delay."

Vince shook his head.

"What?" Kristy arched her brow.

"It's like you're a whole new woman."

She stood up again to resume her watch. "Maybe I am."

She did feel different. More grounded. More herself. She was proud of how she and Ashton had handled their time apart. They'd emerged stronger as a couple, and she felt stronger as an individual, too.

Like she could handle just about anything now that she'd gone through this.

A loud whistle pierced the air, and on the far side of the hangar Jenn, the Family Readiness Officer, stood up on a chair. "Can I have your attention, everyone? The Marines are en route from across base. They should be here in less than ten minutes."

Jenn's last words were drowned out in a flurry of screams. There was a minor stampede as folks surged forward to line up at the open doors.

Kristy's phone vibrated from where she was gripping it in her hand. She glanced down at the display screen.

Ashton: See you soon. ☺

With shaking fingers, she managed to type out a quick message back.

Kristy: Hurry!

Kristy blew out a full breath.

She couldn't believe it was finally happening. Everything she'd dreamed about for the past eight months. All those late nights spent curled up in her bed, watching YouTube videos of military homecomings...it was finally her turn. She smoothed down her navy blue dress and scooted her feet around in her matching wedged heels.

"Come on, Vince. It's go time." Kristy led her brother off to the right side of the crowd, and before she knew it, two white school buses that looked like they'd seen better days appeared in the distance, coming directly for them.

Around her, everyone started clapping and cheering. People held up signs and waved their hands in the air, giving the Marines the boisterous welcome home they deserved.

The buses pulled up so the doors were facing away from where they were all waiting. Kristy couldn't see through the tinted windows, but in the gap beneath the buses and the ground, she could just make out boots debarking.

Kristy began muttering a fervent prayer of gratitude. "Thank you, Jesus. Thank you, Jesus. Thank you, Jesus."

"You okay?" Vince placed his hand on her shoulder.

Happy tears stung the corners of her eyes. "More than okay."

The white buses pulled away, revealing two groups of Marines standing in formation.

Kristy sucked in a breath and clamped her hands over her mouth as around her, everyone went wild, hooting and hollering. She scanned the rows of distant faces as Jenn called for all those who had had a baby while deployed to step forward and be reunited with their Marines first.

It was a sweet tradition, and Kristy probably would have been balling her eyes out if she'd been paying attention. As it was, she was too caught up in frantically searching for Ashton.

They were still too far away, and she couldn't spot him.

Then, all at once, their commander said something, and the Marines responded with a resounding, "Oo-rah!" and broke for-mation.

People started running this way and that, embracing, laughing, and crying.

Kristy hung back, still trying to find Ashton. "Do you see him?" she asked Vince, her heart thudding so hard in her chest, she was afraid it might pop.

"Not yet." Next to her, he stood up on his tiptoes to try to get a better look.

Kristy shifted to her left, and all of a sudden, a group of people parted, and there he was.

He was walking right toward her with a smile to end all smiles on his face.

Kristy took off in a sprint. Ashton opened his arms to her, and she leapt into him. He hoisted her up, and she flung her arms around his neck, circling her legs around his waist.

Through his uniform, Ashton's heart beat out a steady rhythm, and in the most magical way, hers synced perfectly in time.

He stood still, anchoring her tightly to him, and she buried her face into his neck. He smelled like dust and cinnamon, and she drank him in.

Because he was *here*.

She was in his arms.

And it felt even better than she remembered.

When he shifted his grip, she leaned back, looking down into his eyes. "Hi." She grinned at him.

"Hey, you."

She slid down his body, letting her hands rest on his biceps and giving them a quick squeeze. "Nice." She winked as she brought her arms back up to wrap around his neck, running her fingers over the buzz cut hair along his collar.

"Kristy." Ashton said her name with reverence. His gaze burned trails up and down her body and back and forth across her face. It was as if he couldn't see enough of her fast enough. "You are stunning. I love you. So very much."

"I love you, Ashton. Welcome home."

He dipped his head to hers and they met in at achingly sweet kiss—one that was full of promise of a lifetime more to come.

Ashton was home, and in his arms, Kristy was home, too.

Epilogue

ASHTON ~ SEVERAL YEARS LATER

ASHTON SAT SHOULDER-TO-SHOULDER WITH Kristy as they polished off their last bites of dinner—lasagna, of course. Their oldest daughter, Caroline, had left the table five minutes before. He could hear her sweet voice singing a made-up song in his mother-in-law's playroom. Georgia, their other little one, was happily banging her rattle against the tray of her high chair.

A swell of contentment washed over him. He loved his life. He loved his family.

Next to him, Kristy took a sip of her La Croix, and he caught her eye. He leaned over and whispered into her ear. "Still tastes like feet, doesn't it?"

She smirked and side-eyed him. "Are you saying you don't like the taste of it on my lips?"

Ashton hummed. "I like the taste of your lips, period."

Kristy's eyes danced and she turned her head fully so he could kiss her. He was the luckiest man in the world. All these years later, and she still stole his breath.

"Excuse me, but some of us are trying to eat here." Vince pretended to gag at them from across the table before shaking his head. "You're an old married couple now. You're not supposed to act like that."

"Don't knock it until you try it," Ashton chuckled.

"Yeah, and if I'm old, then you must be geriatric," Kristy added.

Vince scrunched up his nose. "You guys are ridiculous. I'm going to play with my favorite humans. People who get me." He pushed back from the table, squeezed his mom's shoulder, scooped up Georgia, and took off for the playroom.

Ashton took the chance to plant another kiss on Kristy's cheek before turning to his mother-in-law.

"The food was amazing, as always, Grandma Paige."

"Ashton, dear. As Vince just established, you've been a part of the family for long enough." Paige's eyes glistened. "You don't have to compliment me on my cooking anymore. Leave your groveling days behind you. Be free!"

Ashton shook his head. "No way. Gotta cement my status as your favorite in-law."

"You're her only in-law at the moment," Kristy said, frowning.

"Too true." Paige's smile dipped. "But not for long."

Kristy arched her brow. "You know something I don't?"

Her mom shook her head. "No. But we can do something about it. I think it's time we...how should I say this? Help him along."

Ashton shot Kristy a side-long glance. There was a gleam in her eyes that he recognized from all the moments in their marriage when she was lining up her ideas and getting ready to make her pitch and convince him to do something. She was pretty much always successful.

He shook his head. "I know that look."

Kristy beamed at him. "What? I am all for this." She placed her hand on his thigh and squeezed. "I just want my brother to be as happy as we are. Don't you?"

"Of course I do. Vince is the best." Ashton couldn't even begin to count the number of times his best friend had come through for him and his family. Babysitting whenever they needed him to. Coming to all of Caroline's kiddie dance recitals. The list went on.

"He really is." Kristy's mom sighed. "But the boy doesn't date. Or he dates, but nothing seems to stick. He hasn't brought a woman around more than once since high school. I don't understand it. There must be something going on."

Kristy nibbled her lip. "So what's your plan?"

"Well." Paige shot a quick look over her shoulder and dropped her voice. "Your cousin is getting married this summer."

Kristy nodded. "They're planning couples events for everything. A couple's bridal shower, a joint bachelor/bachelorette party...the whole shebang."

"I thought we could tell Vince that we have some date suggestions for him. Some women we think he might like." Kristy's mom sat back in her chair and crossed her arms over her chest.

"He'll absolutely hate that."

"Exactly."

"I'm not following." Ashton glanced between the two women. He might have been a part of the family for going on a decade, but he still didn't quite grasp the way his wife and her mom communicated. They always seemed to be on the same page.

Kristy swung her gaze to him. "The only surefire way I know to get Vince to do something is to try to do it for him. He's bound to reject all our suggestions and find a date of his own."

She had a point.

"What do you think?" Paige leaned forward again.

"I think we try it. It's worth a shot."

"Good. Operation Find Vince A Lady is a go."

"On that note"—Ashton pushed away from the table and grabbed Kristy's plate—"you two go relax. I'll do the dishes."

As Paige flitted toward the playroom, Ashton took up his spot at the sink, but before he could turn the faucet on arms wrapped around his waist and the scent of vanilla that was so intrinsically linked to his wife tickled his nose.

"Missed me?" he asked, peering at her over his shoulder.

"Always."

He spun around to hold her properly. "I'm right here."

"I know. I was just thinking about how thankful I am not to have to date any more. Poor Vince," she chuckled.

"He'll be alright, I'm sure." Ashton reached up and tucked a strand of hair behind Kristy's ear.

"I know. We'll make sure of it."

"You're a good sister." Ashton pulled her into a hug, and they stood holding each other for a couple moments before Kristy leaned away.

"You're the best husband. I still choose you. All these years later."

"Ditto. I love you," Ashton said, and then he kissed her.

·❤·❤·❤·❤·❤·

Read on for a sneak peek at *Love at On Deck Café*.

Chapter 1

Julia

Julia Derks stood behind the counter at On Deck Café, but she may as well have been on top of the world. In fact, if she was offered an all-expenses paid trip to anywhere else, she would turn it down. No doubt about it. This place was her pride and joy.

Julia swept a content glance around the café as she poured a cup of coffee for Charlie Pozinski, one of her regulars. Her patrons sat on rich, caramel-colored leather benches flanking tables she had personally salvaged and restored to make one-of-a-kind booths. Mismatched chairs she'd hunted down at estate sales and local antique shops were positioned around the remaining tables in the center of the dining room, infusing the space with an unpretentious, homey vibe. Wide, crank-open windows let in streaks of the summer morning sun, and light dappled the worn wooden floor. A hum of chatter filled the air as stories were shared and laughs exchanged. Julia topped off Charlie's mug with cream and a scoop of sugar—his fixed request.

"Here you go, Charlie." Julia raised her voice to grab the attention of her hard-of-hearing customer, who also happened to be a dear family friend. She offered him a deep smile as he reached for his beverage.

"Thank you kindly." Charlie tipped his hat and walked over to a table of his buddies, the village's crew of older gentlemen, referred to with affection as the *grandpa patrol*. They were all retired and did odd jobs around Mapleton, a small, close-knit community nestled in northeast Wisconsin. The grandpas immediately started heckling Charlie over something or other, and their good-natured laughter echoed through the café, rising up and warming the room like steam from a hot drink.

Yep, there was nowhere else Julia would rather be.

A grin tugged at her lips as the brass bell over the door jingled, and a handsome man she didn't recognize strolled into the café. He looked left and right before his gaze collided with hers. Julia's pulse popped.

Snubbing the flicker of heat working its way up her back, she tossed him a practiced smile before diverting her attention to the counter. She stacked mugs and wiped down the granite work surface so she'd be ready to prepare his order while, out of the corner of her eye, she watched the stranger approach.

The man appeared to be around her age. He wore a crisp, dove-gray button-up shirt that stretched tautly across his broad shoulders. His sandy-blond hair, styled in a way that made it look like it wasn't styled, brushed his collar. A navy-blue tie finished off his business-professional ensemble, the whole thing a contrast in formality to her simple jeans and white t-shirt.

"I'm going to grab another gallon of milk from the kitchen." Amanda Wallace, Julia's best friend and coworker, scooted behind her and disappeared down the hallway as the handsome man arrived at the counter.

"Happy Friday." Julia took up Amanda's position at the register. "What can I get started for you?"

"A large coffee, black. To go, please."

"You got it." Julia entered his order and took the cash payment he fished out of his wallet. Their fingers brushed, and she ignored the shock of electricity at the contact—because, seriously? She wasn't about to let herself become some romance novel cliché in the mere presence of an attractive stranger.

She bent, clearing her throat and tugging a travel cup out from under the counter. "So, what brings you to Mapleton?"

When she rose and met the man's grassy-green eyes, his brow was arched in question.

"How do you know I'm not from Mapleton?"

Julia placed his cup on the counter and swished her hand back and forth, motioning to the crowded café. "I know everyone around here. We have our regulars and the folks who come in occasionally, but you?" She tipped her head, letting her gaze rove over his distinguished-looking face. "I've never seen you before."

The stranger's eyes twinkled, and the sides of his mouth quirked, accentuating the square angles of his jaw and exposing pinprick dimples in either cheek. "Very astute of you."

Whoever this guy was, he was too smooth for his own good—the type of man who knew how good-looking he was and had no shame in flaunting it.

Julia kept her spine straight and gave an easy shrug. "That's me. Astute." She winked, but not—she told herself—in a flirty way. She reached for her pot of coffee. "So again I'll ask, what brings you to Mapleton?"

"I'm here to develop the old paper mill site."

Julia froze mid-pour. With calculated deliberateness, she raised her head to face the man. The collective gasp reverberating through the café informed Julia she'd heard him correctly, but she needed to be sure.

"What did you say?" She gripped the handle on the coffee carafe until her knuckles turned white and waited for him to confirm or deny his business with the mill.

Confusion scampered across the man's face before he masked it with a neutral expression, squared his shoulders, and pulled himself up to his full height.

Julia had a feeling he did so as a show of power—to force her to look up to him. It irked her.

"I said I'm here to develop the mill site. I work for Gabler, Burns, and Associates, the development firm that bought the property. I'm the liaison with the crew who's handling construction."

Judging from his indifferent tone, the stranger had no idea what the mill meant to Mapleton, nor was he interested in learning. Julia stared at him for a second longer, wishing her gaze would zap him into oblivion. When that didn't happen, she broke eye contact and concentrated all of her attention on preparing his drink.

Around her, the café patrons buzzed with displeasure.

"I tell ya what, he's got some nerve!"

Julia recognized Val Marshall's midwestern twang from where she was tucked into a booth near the register with her husband, Dave, and their adult son, Ford.

"It never should have been like this." Charlie's voice, shaking with barely controlled indignation, rose above the rest of the unhappy murmuring coming from the table of grandpas.

At the sound of his raspy outburst, Julia's heart lurched. She snapped on the lid to the coffee cup, and slammed it down on the counter in front of the man. "Here."

The brown liquid sloshed out of the tiny opening, dribbling down the side of the cup and pooling beneath it.

At the same moment, Amanda returned from the kitchen, carrying the milk. She audibly inhaled at Julia's lack of hospitality...for good reason. Never before had Julia made such a scene in front of her customers. She was a professional, after all, and she didn't have a confrontational bone in her body. But this was different. This had to do with the mill.

"Um, thanks, I guess." The man reached for a stack of napkins.

Julia turned away from him, her skin prickling with irritation. She wasn't going to give him any more of her time or emotional bandwidth. He wasn't worth it. If she never saw him again, it would be too soon.

"Hey," he raised his deep voice, and even with her back to him, she could tell he was trying to recapture her attention.

Julia ground her jaw. Didn't he realize she was trying to make a statement here? Still, she couldn't just ignore a paying customer. She glanced briskly over her shoulder, her long ponytail whipping the side of her face. "What?" she snapped.

"Is there something I should know about the mill? Like you pointed out, I'm not from around here."

The smirk he shot her was a clear attempt at charm. It was as if he thought she was willingly going to spill all of Mapleton's secrets.

Julia balled up her hands at her sides. "It's nothing someone like you would understand."

Without giving him a chance to say another word, she spun on her heel, walked past an open-mouthed Amanda, and strode into the storage closet behind the bar.

A moment later, the bell over the door jingled, signaling the stranger's departure, and the conversation in the dining room reached fever pitch. Julia groaned, slumping against the closet wall and trying to reign in her galloping heart.

In a village the size of Mapleton, it would take about ten minutes for word to spread that Julia had confronted the new guy about the mill development. Most people wouldn't complain, but Julia didn't like the attention.

And if her mom caught wind of her manners, she'd be scolded as if she were seven and not twenty-seven.

Julia sighed and tugged her shoulders back. There was no use hiding. The man was gone—hopefully for good.

She made up her mind to do her best to avoid him for however long he was in Mapleton, which shouldn't be too difficult to do. He had the sort of dazzling face that attracted all the light in a room. Not that she cared about that, but she was sure he'd stick out in a crowd, and when he did, she'd walk in the opposite direction.

Julia found a fresh dishcloth on the shelf and returned to the bar, setting to work scrubbing the counter as if her life depended on it.

"Woah. Take it easy there, boss." Amanda held up her hand, giving Julia the universal *stop* sign.

"I am taking it easy." Julia bent closer to the counter and rubbed back and forth over a tiny spot.

"Right. Come on. Give me the rag before you scrub the finish right off of the stone."

"Very funny." Julia made a face but stood upright and conceded the cloth. "I'm fine. Everything's fine."

Amanda dangled the rag from her finger and cocked her head. "Okay, then." She stretched out the words, exaggerating her skepticism. "If you say so."

One of their regular customers came in and saved Julia from having to say anything more on the subject.

Amanda turned her attention to the register and smiled at the middle-aged woman who bustled forward. "Hi, Susan. Do you want your usual?"

"You better believe it." Susan Tillersand plopped her oversized purse on the counter to retrieve her payment.

Julia got to work fulfilling the order, half listening as Susan gave them the play-by-play of how she was nearly rear-ended the other night coming out of the ballpark.

Most days, Julia loved hearing about what her customers were up to. It kept the job fresh. But right now, her mind felt fuzzy, like an out-of-focus camera. Fortunately, she'd whipped up so many lattes since opening the café that at this point she could do it half asleep with one hand tied behind her back. She tried to regain her composure as she waited for the milk to steam. But her conversation with the arrogant developer continued to eat away at her until it felt like steam was escaping her ears.

Julia took a calming breath and added a shot of espresso into the to-go mug before pouring the steamed milk over the top of it. Dolloping a scoop of foam onto the drink, she sprinkled on some cinnamon and *wah-lah!*

"Here you are, Susan."

On the outside, she was as perky as could be. After all, Julia could fake it with the best of them. *Fake it 'til you make it*—that was her motto. She'd gotten this business off the ground doing just that. And it was a business that depended on her regulars.

"Thanks, Jules." The mom of three smiled. She took a sip then closed her eyes and moaned. "I'm going to need this today. Swimming lessons, then straight to baseball practice, home for lunch, then an afternoon of tot time, and a soccer game for the oldest tonight."

Julia grinned. "You should have asked for a large drink."

"No, then I'd get all jittery. Life is crazy, but I wouldn't have it any other way." With a wave of her fingers, Susan turned and left through the front door.

The crowd in the coffee shop had thinned a bit with folks leaving for work. Daniel Smith took up his usual position by the front window, laptop open and wireless headphones in. A couple years behind Julia in school, he now worked as a freelance writer, and he used the café as his office. He was a great customer—friendly, well-mannered, and a good tipper. Since they spent most of their days together, Julia considered him a friend. She caught his eye and waved.

Satisfied everything was in order, Julia decided to check on the outdoor space and give herself a chance to reset. "I'm heading out to the deck."

Amanda nodded, and Julia cut down the hallway along the west side of the building where a door opened onto the café's outdoor seating area. She caught a faint whiff of coffee beans as the door swung shut behind her, but on the deck, the smell of freshly cut grass prevailed.

In Julia's opinion, her deck was the crown jewel of On Deck Café. It overlooked Sunrise Park, a massive expanse of trees and trails that was also home to the village baseball diamonds and soccer fields. For those who weren't interested in up-close-and-personal seats to the games, the deck at On Deck Café made for a clear, though distant, viewing spot. For others, it was a comfortable and friendly place to come and rehash the game—to celebrate a victory or to drown a defeat with some caffeinated beverages.

Around the deck, blue-and-white-striped umbrellas were strategically positioned to shield the sun. Flower boxes hung from the wooden railings, stuffed with sun-loving petunias and snapdragons in a rainbow of bold colors.

Julia walked along the railings, stopping to deadhead the flowers that needed care. The morning sun warmed the back of her neck, and signs of the day ahead swirled all around her. A field maintenance worker chalked new foul ball lines in the grass of the field closest to the café. Another man ran a weed-eater around the dugouts. A couple of senior ladies pumped their arms back and forth as they power-walked on the path circling the ball-fields, their windbreakers billowing in the early morning breeze and their mouths flapping in time. Mourning doves warbled in the trees, and the faint echo of the rushing Squirrel River beyond the park made it to her ears. These sights and sounds were the fabric of her day. They reminded her of all that was good in life and in her little town.

Yet, even as she stood in her favorite spot, Julia couldn't quite get rid of the sour taste in her mouth left by the stranger who'd stopped by the café.

Any mention of the old mill nettled her. It had been ten years, but the memory of the day she found out about the mill shutting down would stay with her forever.

The party line of the powers-that-be was, "It's not personal; it's business."

Julia loathed that sentiment.

Doing good business was personal. Separating the two was impossible because personal and business were two sides of the same coin. You couldn't have a business without being a decent person or without thinking about the people affected by your actions. That was why what she'd built with the café was a business that was like a beloved friend. She could be proud of that.

"Hey, girl. Can I get a hand?"

Julia turned to see Amanda motioning to her from the entrance to the shop. Her best friend stood like Rosie the Riveter, hands on her hips, curly auburn hair tied up with a cute blue bandana. Her fitted chambray shirt peeked out from under the black apron she wore as part of the café uniform.

"Of course!" Julia inhaled the summer air one more time, smoothing down her own apron before heading inside with a smile on her face.

She wouldn't let some good-for-nothing man ruin a lovely day.

Dear Readers,

Thank you for reading *Choosing Love*. I hope you enjoyed a taste of Mapleton, in all its sweet, small-town glory! Ashton and Kristy have lived in my head for a long time, so getting them out onto the page and letting you meet them is extra special.

If you originally read this book as part of my newsletter promotion, I hope you spotted the additions. I had so much fun building the story out!

While *Choosing Love* is not autobiographical, my husband did spend five years in the Marine Corps, so I drew on the memories of our experience as a military family to flesh out some of the dynamics of Kristy and Ashton's relationship.

If you love these two as much as I do, you can see where they are now in *Love at On Deck Café*. And be on the lookout for Vince's story soon! It's one of my very favorites.

Thank you for supporting my dream of filling the world with love and stories. Happy reading!

With love,
Leah

Also by Leah Dobrinska

The Mapleton Series

Love at On Deck Café
Good To Be Home
Together With You

The Larkspur Library Mystery Series

Death Checked Out

About the Author

Leah Dobrinska is the author of the Larkspur Library Mysteries, a cozy mystery series set in the Wisconsin Northwoods, and the Mapleton novels, a series of award-winning standalone small town romances. She earned her degree in English Literature from UW-Madison where she was awarded the Dean's Prize and served as a Writing Fellow.

Leah lives in Wisconsin with her husband and their gaggle of kids. When she's not writing, handing out snacks, or visiting local parks, Leah enjoys reading and running. Find out more about Leah, join her newsletter community, and connect with her through her website, leahdobrinska.com.

Acknowledgments

All glory to God, now and forever.

If you're reading this, I owe you a whole heap of thanks. There are so many amazing books out there, so the fact that you made it to the end of mine is not something I take for granted. Thank you for giving Kristy, Ashton, and the entire Mapleton crew a chance. I hope you enjoyed your visit!

To my cover designer extraordinaire, Ana Voicu, at Books-Design. You hit it out of the park...again! Thanks for continuing to lend your incredible talent to the art that brings Mapleton to life.

To the writing community and bookstagrammers I've had the pleasure of meeting. Thank you for championing my stories. You are some of the kindest humans, and I'm so grateful to know you. All the stars!

To those serving in the armed forces and to their families. I see you, and I'm so grateful for your continued sacrifices. Semper fi.

To my family and friends. You have been so supportive of me forever. I couldn't do this without you. I love you to the moon and back.

To my kids. I've forever grateful to be your mom, and I love you more than words can say.

To Nick. Always I will choose you. Thanks for choosing me, too.

Kristy's Deployment Playlist

1. *Can't Help Falling in Love*, Hailey Reinhart

2. *Iris*, The Goo Goo Dolls

3. *New Year's Day*, Taylor Swift

4. *Fight Song*, Rachel Platten

5. *You Are In Love*, Taylor Swift

6. *First Flight Home*, Jake Miller

7. *How You Get the Girl*, Taylor Swift

8. *Nothing Without Love*, Nate Ruess

9. *Come Back, Be Here*, Taylor Swift

10. *I Will Always Return*, Bryan Adams

11. *Photograph*, Ed Sheeran

12. *Livin' On A Prayer*, Bon Jovi

13. *It's Gonna Be Me*, *NSYNC

14. *Home*, American Authors

www.ingramcontent.com/pod-product-compliance
Lightning Source LLC
Chambersburg PA
CBHW031005210726
48290CB00007B/2486